AF397447

VIKTOR KOROBKO

The Story of Life… and Not Just That

novum pro

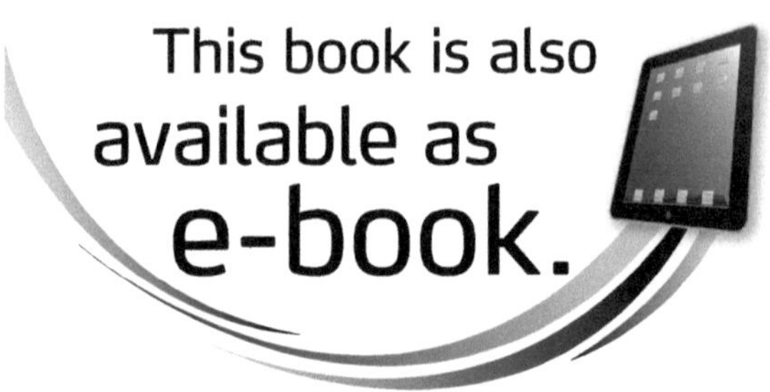

All rights of distribution, including via film, radio, and television, photomechanical reproduction, audio storage media, electronic data storage media, and the reprinting of portions of text, are reserved.

Printed in the European Union on environmentally friendly, chlorine- and acid-free paper.

© 2020 novum publishing

ISBN 978-3-99064-895-7
Editing: Ashleigh Brassfield, DipEdit
Cover design, layout & typesetting: novum publishing

www.novum-publishing.co.uk

I wish to say "Thank You" to Charlotte Foster, for her outstanding job of interpretation the majority of those texts originally written in Russian language, into English. To John Wilkinson for initial editing of "The Story of Life". And so to "Novum Publishing" for their great work of editing. Without your time and attention to the details – this collection of novels would have never appeared in English.

Contents

SEVEN

"The next day the Romans climbed up to Masada, and when they discovered the piles of corpses, they took no joy in the sight of their slain enemies, but were frozen in silence, struck by their greatness of spirit and steadfast contempt for death."
(Flavius Josephus (from the words of two unidentified women and five children, who survived))

One

Each day is the last, each day is the last, each day is the last, each day is the last, each day is the last, each day is the last, each day is the last. Each day, if only for a fraction of a second, this thought enters your head – between breathing in and breathing out.

Two

There are two of them in the room. They are smoking and drinking from cups. Their wings are extraordinarily beautiful, an awesome sight.

"What is the difference between dreams and reality? What do you think?"

"Well, just between you and me… Dreams give us wings to fly. In our dreams, we create miracles. In our dreams, we are free, and we can go wherever and be whoever we like!"

"But in reality, we create life. Isn't that a miracle? A dream is gone in an instant, but wakefulness is a hard slog. You favour dreams because dreams are an illusion and that's the easy route."

"In reality, we catch up on sleep. In our dreams we come alive. If it is truly the easy way out, why haven't they learned how to control dreams? They like to keep reality under control, but so far, they are powerless against dreams!"

"I don't quite agree with that statement. We act in the name of the life granted to us by our Father. We are small particles of it, and we constitute it. We act according to His will. This is still reality, even if we spend part of it asleep. Dreams are just an extension – reality is the essence of life!"

"What makes you so sure that our Father didn't create all this chaos in a dream? Will you ask Him when you see Him?"

"The Bible, my brother – you know very well that all the answers are there in the Bible. But I think we've hung around here long enough. Finish your cigarette and let's get to work."

"We didn't write the Bible, nor did our Father. But you're right, it's time to get back to work. That's something we all have in common – everyone has a job to do."

They smiled at each other, walked out of the room and vanished with a flap of their wings.

Three

The fledgling crow was pitiful with its broken wing. "It won't ever be able to fly again," Olav said, holding it in the palm of his hand. His bearded friends sneered.

Somebody said: "Olav, you need to find a wife. You're ready to jump on a crow. I bet you twisted its wing just to stop it flying off to another..." There was friendly laughter from the bearded hulks, as they landed on the shore.

"I feel sorry for the poor little thing," Olav thought to himself. "He can't fly like his brothers, he's totally on his own."

Walking out into a clearing, Olav bent down and placed the fledgling on the grass. "I'll get you something to eat in a minute," he said to the bird. "Wait for me here."

After a while they returned, covered in blood and ashes. It was an easy job. The folk at the monastery didn't know how to fight, so they fell quickly. Their blood was now nourishing the hills. Olav's companions were carrying some sort of church plate, four silver crosses, engravings depicting some figures and a chalice made of silver and gold plate. That was their entire haul. He was also carrying something in his hand. It was dripping heavily onto the ground… The monastery was burning – there was nobody left alive.

At the clearing Olav searched all around, but he couldn't find the bird anywhere. "He's gone? OK, I'll leave it for him – he might come back later."

He placed the dismembered hand next to a stone; young fingers which had tried to clutch onto life for the last time. But life had slipped away, leaving them crooked and growing cold. "It's like a new wing for the bird," Olav thought, smiling, as he walked to the boat. He found this idea amusing, and as he walked away, he considered that he had kept his promise to the little crow. "It's a pity he went off – he didn't believe me. But it would have been great to see him again. He's just like me – totally on his own."

Four

"But who was better, the Greeks or the Romans? Who made history greater? Who gave more to the world?

"Socrates and Plato or Seneca and Marcus Aurelius? Whose empire was stronger in its heyday? Who, who??

"What an excruciating choice!"

The man just couldn't decide, but then he said to himself: "I know!" He took a bottle of Greek Kormilitsa and an Italian Barabesco and pushed his trolley to the check-out. "Now we have equilibrium![1] No more intolerable questions."

---

1 Equilibrium from the Latin "aequus" – equal, "libra" – scales.

Five

The Holy Father, Adam Bezhinsky, seemed calm on the outside, but his head and his heart were in turmoil. For several days in a row he had been drinking wine in the evenings, quite an expensive, dry wine, which he had found in the neighbouring grocery. He was tormented by a question to which he could find no answer.

"The Lord created the Land and Sea… and all living creatures – that's a fact. The Bible says that the Lord did that… But the Bible doesn't say where the Lord came from. And what if…?" He was afraid to ask this question out loud, his body in a sweat. "And what if the Lord was sent by someone above Him? Somebody who created the Lord?"

He could not find the answer and was frightened to ask the senior confessor, feeling this question gnawing, like a worm, at his conscience. The foundations of his concept of existence were being rocked by a tremor from outside. He was becoming more and more enslaved by the thought. His glass was half full. Adam continued to drink, alone. The wine unravelled his thoughts.

"Praise the Lord for creating the vine and teaching us sinners how to make wine. The sea and the stars were, of course, a great feat, but what would this civilisation have done without wine?! Wine was a massive breakthrough.

"A more groundbreaking invention than the creation of the Internet. What can you do with the Internet? You can ask it questions! But with wine you can pose questions to Almighty God himself, to whoever you like. And you can… Yes, but all the same, somebody sent You to us, oh Lord!

"Where do You come from?"

Six

A small boy was picking his nose and watching the world go by. The street where he lived was not in the best part of town – it was just an ordinary street. But he was special, this little lad. From the balcony on the fifth floor of his drab block of flats, from the small litter-strewn balcony, he looked down onto the street below.

What was unusual about his world view was that he did not see people as ordinary homo sapiens[2] see them.

After his father abandoned the family, and his mother started to drink and to beat him and his brother… and after she once beat him half to death and they took her away for treatment, and they, the boys, were left to live with Auntie Angela… after that, he began to see people, animals and the world differently.

People appeared to him as if they were composed entirely of light. Often he could not even make out the outline of their faces, for the light washed away their individuality. Everyone seemed to look the same – as if they all shared one face.

And it was not just people. Food appeared to him as light, like a flickering burst of energy – sometimes dim, sometimes bright. Water seemed like a slurry of light, glowing with different hues. Smells and voices were somehow strange, while the outlines of solid objects and their contents were luminescent.

Some people seemed to shine in a special way. He did not know what to call such light, for he didn't have the words to describe it. But this strange light made his heart beat stronger – sometimes with anxiety, sometimes with joy.

Sometimes, light would speak to him in the form of a person.

And now he could see a light flying towards him. It looked like a dolphin… Just imagine – a dolphin, flying through the sky as if it were the ocean!

The dolphin flew up quite close and the little boy, Billy, saw emptiness in its eyes. There was nothing there…nothing came from them. There was just a warm outer shell, a kind of peace. It wasn't frightening; there was simply a sensation of approaching emptiness.

"Hello. Do you know where I can find someone called Auntie Mendl around here? They told me you could help. I have to

2 Homo sapiens (Latin) – wise man

deliver some news to her," said the light-being as it neared the balcony where Billy was sitting. It seemed as if the creature was smiling at him.

Billy started to shake his head and said: "She's downstairs. I don't know exactly where. I'm too small to know everything."

The dolphin laughed.

"Qua, qua, qua…" he made a quacking sort of sound. "That's a funny thing to say. Of course you know, otherwise I wouldn't have asked you. You have already helped, and when we call for you and I bring you the news, you will become one of us. You will be a guardian of the secret."

The little boy was pleased. He was proud of the fact that he was to be entrusted with an important job. And he asked the light-dolphin-creature: "What sort of secret?"

"A secret is secret for a reason — so that you don't go blabbing about it. I have to hurry because I am on an errand. I'll see you again."

The special little boy, Billy, was extremely excited, and he resolved not to tell anyone about this conversation or the meeting.

Twenty minutes later he looked down at the street again. He could hear shouting and there was a commotion. The usual thing.

The boy didn't pay any attention to the play of light down below… He was strangely contemplative, without any clear thoughts in his head. He was calm and agitated at the same time; his eyes were empty and gazed down from the balcony, while the thoughts in his head sparked his imagination.

Just a few thoughts slipped across the surface of his mind like pond skaters: "A secret! Guardian of the secret!" Anybody would be excited by this!

Then he went back into the room. It was a small dirty room, full of different-coloured light-objects. Aunt Angela was cooking something on the stove and chatting on her mobile phone.

He heard the words: "Yes. Today. Only about half an hour ago! Yes, our Mendl was crossing the road and she just dropped down dead! She looked up at the sky, as if she had seen something, and dropped down dead! Poor old soul. I feel sorry for her, there isn't even anyone to bury her, but let the bloody council pay for her death now. Nobody pays for you in life, but at least the old girl has got her own back in death…"

Auntie Angela laughed her dry smoker's laugh.

Little Billy stood pensively in the room. "So it's out – that's the secret! Somebody always has to pay for death! I will ask him next time he comes flying by. I guess this "bloody council" must be very rich, paying for the death of every single person! I wonder what message he was taking to Auntie Mendl? Maybe he was late getting to her because he stopped off with me, then she took it and died! I must suss it all out next time."

Seven

A girl was playing the piano to the audience in the hall. She was playing Frederic Chopin's Waltz No. 1, the "Grande Valse Brillante". She always played so passionately that the adults called her a child prodigy…she was indifferent to praise.

The music rang out: Passion and simplicity. Vigour and melancholy. The girl played and saw nothing except for herself in her blue and white silk kimono with the cherry tree, Mount Fuji and the dragon… And her friend, her real, true friend.

This friend was a katana[3], which she called "Gentle Death". They had already supported each other for a long time. "Gentle Death" had never betrayed her and never abandoned her. It was an extension of the girl in her battles.

The girl's hands touched the keys, which created a sound in intricate combination with the instrument's other mechanisms. The sound filled the celestial spheres. There was whispering from the people in the hall, and the pedal creaked slightly when the girl pressed it with her foot.

---

3 Katana– a long Japanese sword

She was focussed on her battle. Nothing else interested her. She was an ordinary Ukrainian girl who had read a lot of books and had wanted to learn the art of sword fighting ever since she had been diagnosed with a tumour. Or, more consciously, since Oleg Kulbida, the boy she had fallen for, had moved to another part of the town three years ago – transferred from her school to another and found himself a new girlfriend.

She wanted to cut herself off from the past, or to cut the ugly head off this banal and stupid past.

And for this she needed a sword.

Of all the swords she had read about in books and seen in films, she liked the Japanese ones the best. They had class and spirit. The ones they used for killing in "Kill Bill"; a trashy film, but wicked swords!

She told her parents about her wish – for a long time she was too afraid to ask, but then, brimming with determination, she came out with it. Her parents just shook their heads. They didn't understand that she needed this to become strong!

Her parents could not conceive of it – it was too dangerous, and very odd: their daughter, at thirteen years old, wanted to set out on a military path! The piano – that's where your success lies, child…

She played with the katana. It was great when "Gentle Death" cut through the air and sang its song, clashing in battle with the blades of her adversaries. Strength and steel. The blood of her enemies flowed from the blade, but this did not particularly worry her. They were vulgar and surly people, who wanted to lock her up. To hide her away from her true friend! Of course, all of this dissolved into the air, appeared again and disappeared, fluttered and then vanished. It was just like the vibrations in the air which she produced with her fingers. Her heart beat faster, no doubt in time with the music. She was calm and seemed detached, yet her eyes gleamed with passion when she slashed the world with her music. She was going into the unknown, and "Gentle Death" was with her.

"Each day is the last," pounded in her head, and she lived in the sounds of the music, in the sounds of her battle.

"Just look at her eyes," her teacher whispered to the person sitting next to her, "So much passion!" And she continued, with sincerity: "She's a lovely, gentle girl. And so talented! A pianist sent from God, and such an awful illness… Her poor parents are really suffering!"

Odessa, 16–18 May 2015

THE STORY OF LIFE

I confess: I hated paying taxes. Wherever I have lived and worked before, I have tried to avoid it, to escape it, or to defer it as much as possible.

I liked to get the cash into my hands, rather than fill and feed those cards or bank accounts. Some people called me old fashioned! Others said I have been poisoned with the ideas of anarchy, and my way would lead me to crime or criminals one day.

"Well," thought I, "not bad: being old fashioned is not a crime."

For your information, the heavyweight champion Rocky Marciano also accepted only cash, in a time of cheques! So I was not a great anachronism, I just loved to sense the cash. Nothing personal – with all those scandals, schemes and suicidal tendencies in today's business-like supreme financial spheres, I have simply lost any trust in the banks, their plastic cards and their e-money.

As for the route to crime – you know, I was not going to enter into politics or to wage wars, and thus I felt no closer to criminals than, say, to the Martians.

It depends how you classify it and what you consider to be a crime!

My way was almost as innocent as the wolf's in the wild forest. The wolf wants to eat – would you penalise him for that?! The wolf wants to be free in his choice of what to eat; so do I.

For me, the freedom, so much talked about and advertised in America over recent centuries, is an ability to live my own life with no pressure on me from all those loafers who tax me and suck from my pocket to create all that nonsense they call "stability".

"Hey, you guys at the top, d'you hear me now?! I don't need your stability! It becomes way too expensive for a guy like me! Ok, call me what you will, but I consider myself a 'cautious tax payer'; too cautious to follow every bill I receive, and that's why I try to receive as few bills as possible. Easy living when you are bill-less!"

One day, going about my lovely smuggling job, I crossed the border with Mexico to meet a client of mine, to whom I was delivering … books! Yeah, a strange business.

He had opened a sort of public library in his home. A large house, lots of space, and it was like a kingdom for the books. He did not let the people take the books outside, but he let them read in the reading hall of his castle.

With such a large space and just a trickle of visitors, from those who could read in English, loved to read, and could find the time to come and read, the whole idea of this client of mine lacked any commercial sense.

However, my client was solvent. And, ah, let me introduce the man: Silvio De Granito.

Normally, he sends me an order by fax only, as he doesn't trust the internet. I collect the books for him in LA, or order them via the internet from New York, Seattle, or even from Canada or England from time to time.

Once I complete the order – I cross the border and deliver the goods. And he pays me triple the price or sometimes even more! A very generous man with a very strange business, but you'll find it interesting in a moment.

He told me a story, a life story. There was a storm outside and I asked if I could stay at his house for the night, until the weather calmed down. He liked the idea and immediately agreed. It felt like he had been missing good company for a while.

With some whiskey consumed, in an hour or so we saw that the storm had just become stronger, and there was no hurry for me to rush even in the morning, so we had plenty of time to talk.

Silvio, (I am still not sure if that was his real name) told me his story, and if someone believes it the way that I did, then I am happy to share what he told me!

He was a gangster, and well, the prophecy was true – the one about love for cash. By the way, Rocky Marciano who I mentioned before, also had his way to the criminals, so the theory shows a trend. But people are people, good or bad – they all love cash but only a few will admit it openly.

Silvio and his gang planned and executed seven armed robberies of jewellery shops in the New York area and then got caught by police and the FBI. He was sentenced (thanks to his lawyers) to eleven years in prison. But his organisation survived and continued to generate income for when freedom came, while he received accommodation and food from the State.

After he had served his term and was released, he met with the former crew. But times had changed, you know …

What I mean, is that as per the criminal code, they owed him his share, a sort of a pension fund. Part of it had already been spent on food, drink, light drugs, and other pleasures of life, since all of that had been supplied and delivered to Silvio while he used the cell paid by budget.

Now, all money transactions had become complicated. Bankers were no longer reliable and were likely to share the data with the Federals, so big cash transfers attracted too much attention.

But he insisted on getting the cash. Like me, he loved to see de facto money.

His boys consulted with a nice guy, obviously a smart one – a lawyer who was used by their organization (for the sake of causing no harm to myself, I have left the real names off the deck, you know!) and Mr. Shemkis (the lawyer) advised them to use a private foundation in Belize to remit the cash as a grant for some piece of art or a book et cetera.

The book seemed, most of all, a legit idea.

Silvio had to write a book to get his cash, so his brotherhood found him a young writer from New Jersey who had written some novels but could not sell them well.

They found their way to him and then their cash did the same. So, speaking openly, a young writer, let's call him Andrew here, sold them the rights to the book he had written along with the authorship. Hey presto! Silvio became an author!

All was fine – the transfer proceeded safely but to prove the story was very true, his brotherhood convinced a small publisher to print a few thousand hard copies that went to the bookstores.

Again, the cash made it happen, otherwise who would be aware? No name, no number…a new author. All of a sudden, the book sold well!

Wow!, the orders were coming in thick and fast, which was a serious concern for our author, as he wanted to take his time and not to become an advertisment with reporters following his every step. He had been eleven long years in a public institution, so it was absolutely natural that he wanted to stay away from being photographed and interviewed.

He hired a manager and Mr. Shemkis protected his rights and his privacy from a legal standpoint, and for some time, life stablilized. Silvio thought he was a lucky guy and that it was a case of "God's will' to pay the bill after his years of service to the State!

But Andrew, the young writer, had other ideas. He also hired lawyers, and they smelled blood! They lodged a claim against Silvio in the courts and demanded that he disclosed the name of the actual author, Andrew Bolshowitz, who wrote the book.

After almost a year, those hyenas, as Silvio called his opponents, managed to prove the authorship of the book (apparently, one of the early originals was found at one publisher's house… the legacy of one of Andrew's early efforts to find a way to success) creating quite a problem for Silvio.

His solicitor told him to go speak to the journalists as silence only made things worse. As you may imagine, the FBI, knowing Silvio, were showing a lot of interest in the Charity Foundation which had paid almost a million dollars in 'grants' to the gangster, who was now involved in a scandal over the fake authorship of a famous book!

Silvio started to give interviews. He spoke about his hard life in prison and how he spent the long days and nights writing the book…

A few of the former prison officers, who had known Silvio for years, were recipients of luxury Swiss watches and confirmed, "Yeah, this guy spent all his time in prison, writing his story…"

And in public, Silvio showed good manners and gentle speech, was modest and dedicated to his art, so he looked to the journalists like the samaritan victim of unprecedented lies.

Andrew, his opponent, on the other hand behaved aggressively, and the journalists made him out to be a gangster-like person; disregarding the fact he had no relation at all to the Mafia before this story began. Again, cash was king!

Finally, Silvio started to get the upper hand in this battle, and his brotherhood paid a visit to Andrew Bolshowitz to persuade him to accept an "amicable solution". The guy gave up… which was understandable in the circumstances!

The Mafia team celebrated the victory, but it was, unfortunately, a bit premature, for after a few days, when the court convened to rule against him, Mr. Bolshowitz made it all just a bit more complicated! He took his revenge on Silvio and his organisation by committing suicide… leaving paperwork explaining "who is who" in the game and blaming Silvio and the Mafia for "destroying the Life and Hope of America"!

There was a huge campaign against Silvio on the TV, and the FBI visited him for an "interview" again. Knowing he had to act really fast, he approached his banker and asked him to cash whatever was left in his account.

The banker was scared, but Silvio was prepared, and the banker received a phone call, and heard his wife begging him to execute all "their orders" otherwise "they will execute me". The cash was handed over.

Silvio was due to pay a visit to the FBI the next day, for questioning, but instead, overnight, he secretly joined a truck driver who was delivering his cargo to Mexico, and, accompanied by his cash, was next morning beyond US legislation.

Later, his body was found in a burned out car somewhere in Boston, and of course his Mafia connections and prison relations were remembered by newsmakers. The cash made him a dead man, while he was drinking tequila at his *hacienda*.

"You know," he said, "I never intended to harm this guy, Andrew, but he did it to himself. He just refused to compromise with us and this was taken as a betrayal from our side. But I confess, it was never personal – the whole dirty job was done by greedy lawyers and journalists!"

I took the liberty of asking Silvio "What was the book about?!"

"Oh, it was about a young author who so much wanted to be famous, that he sold his soul to the Devil. And then he dies in the end … the name of the book was "The Story of Life", as the main hero's name was John Life."

His face took on a sad smile as he continued, before we finished the bottle and our talk: "You know, man, I was lucky in life, and the other guys did not have the same luck. I felt a bit guilty about Mr. Bolshowitz, and all that nonsense, so I changed my name here in Mexico and am no longer associated with any author of this book. As I told you before – both authors are dead, officially dead, completely dead!

"I have started a new life here, bought this house and welcomed a lot of books into it. I find myself in good company, among wise people…Plato, Hemingway, Tolstoy, Kipling and an army of other good names. But sometimes I miss a life I wasted, and once a year I find a guy like you to tell this story to. Fresh ears. Nobody believes me, but who cares! It was on another planet, and it's late now for any more talking, so let's go and get some sleep. Ciao."

I returned to the US the following day, and standing by my house in the suburbs of LA, I could not shake off the impression this story had made on me. I felt myself a witness to a crime but also a listener to a good lesson! I found a copy of "The Story of Life" and have read it.

I must say: the real story behind it was way more interesting, and what came to mind was that Silvio requested those books to be delivered by that kind of courier service for a special reason! He could have made all his orders through Amazon, or other sources and that would not have raised any suspicion. But he wanted me (or someone like me) to invite in and to listen to his story, because he had to find someone who was somehow connected to literature, illegal activity and the United States of America, to get the picture well enough. My consciousness tried to find me an answer as to why, and I finally understood, a few days later, one summer's morning. He wanted to have the story continued, to let the readers know what was behind the official truth.

The Mafia kept him alive because he spoke no word to the FBI and disappeared just in time. His brotherhood made a gesture and misled the Feds from his trail using a decoy body, dead already, and a car to be burned out in Boston. That was their final contribution to Silvio, instead of simply finding him there in Mexico and silencing him for ever.

But you know, Mafia men, they always talk about reputation, and possibly that was one of the reasons Silvio wanted to rehabilitate himself in the eyes of the public! You see, during his brief role as the author of a book he had never written, he was loved by the public. It changed his life and he was looking to pass on his story, his legacy, to someone else on this earth, to ensure that it continued and was known. And that seems to be one instance where just the power of cash may be useless.

And here's my story!

Imagine: I changed my job afterwards; I rented this bar and I sell drinks to my clients to generate an income for living. A tiny drinking station, called "Eddie's Place". Things are going well, and I pay my taxes. That is no longer a big issue for me. I may pay them since I have a great mission ahead, still to be completed.

I use my free time to write a book, which I hope will reach lots of readers once it is published. And you may guess what it is about – a life story, as usual.

PARABLE OF THE DRAGON

Once, long ago, my dad invited Andrei over to visit. Andrei was tall and well-built, and he had a black belt in karate.

Dad and Andrei were having a drink and talking about something or other. I don't know what.

Before he left, Andrei told me a parable.

"There was once a monastery in the mountains. There were very few in the congregation because it was so high up. The monks gathered brushwood and carried it down to sell in the villages below. They also caught fish from a beautiful lake next to the monastery.

"'If only I could do something to let the whole of Japan see how beautiful the lake is,' thought one of the monks to himself.

"And so it happened that one of the monks, without any malicious intent or self-interest whatsoever, started to tell the people in the village at the foot of the mountain that in the fourth month, Uzuki, a Dragon would appear from the waters of the lake. He could be seen, and anyone who caught sight of him would enjoy success and good health for the whole year ahead.

"Well, this tale gradually spread around the whole empire. It was embellished with all sorts of new details, and one day it came back to the monastery. Thousands of people travelled from all corners of the country to get a glimpse of the Dragon.

"What a wonderful time that was! There were fireworks, rice dishes and baked fish... it all created a joyous atmosphere and generated profit.

"But the awaited day came, as described in the legend: 'And so at midnight the Dragon will emerge from the waters of the lake.'

"The monks knew that the Dragon did not exist. But they also knew how much the visitors needed him – and how much the monastery needed him.

"So they joined hands and prayed. But their prayer was not sufficient, so they announced that if all the visitors were to join hands and start to pray, the Dragon would appear. The people started to pray, and when the prayer gained force, it created the Dragon and he emerged from the waters of the lake.

"This parable shows how weak the Dragon is inside each of us individually, but how strong it becomes if everyone makes a concerted effort to create something together."

Not long afterwards, Andrei was killed in a shoot-out in the street. Bullets fly wherever their master sends them – all targets are the same to them.

RESOLVE

I saw another dolphin. It looked quite big, but its skin had started to go dull in the morning sun. Something had happened after the storm, and the creature was on the shore. The storm had raged on the island for two days, and at a few narrow points the waves had leapt across strips of land from one side to the other. That was the type of storm they experienced there!

I had counted three of its kind that morning, cast out by the sea. Two of its fellow creatures had died, but this one was still alive.

I dragged it into the water. It was ever so heavy, but I was sturdy back then and plenty strong enough.

The dolphin circled in the water, jerking its tail in a peculiar way; then, when it had swum a short way out from the shore, it came back onto the sand. By itself. It accelerated, and in a flash it was back on the beach.

It had probably already decided to die, and how can you counter such resolve? I'm not joking, this isn't what usually happens when they want the opposite – to survive! Then they thrash about, squirm, make a din and generally use all the energy they can muster. In this case, there was simply a sense of peace.

When I went back half an hour later, I noticed that there was barely a glimmer of life left in the dolphin. It looked at me through the film covering its eyes. I felt sorry for it and desperately wanted to help it survive. But even then, it was quite clear that it would not waver from its intention…

THREE SHORT TALES ABOUT SOUTHERNERS, FOREIGN CARS, MILITARY CUNNING AND A SPECIAL USE FOR ALCOHOL

One

In the early nineties, after pulling off a couple of successful business deals, an uncle of mine turned up with a car. Not just any old car, but a foreign-made diesel off-roader. When he appeared in the town square of Chernomorka in his motor, the drunks, workers and shopkeepers all stared at him, much as the Native Americans probably stared at Columbus when he brought them beads and Christianity.

On starting up, the engine would let out a formidable roar, and the steed of steel and glass would travel through the streets and alleyways, and off-road along so-called "tracks"…

Once, the monster vehicle started faltering and playing up. My uncle called out a friend who was a motor mechanic, and after poking about a bit, he said: "Listen, our diesel is lousy – the engine might be made by hand, but our fuel is made by foot. That's all there is to it."

They smoked a cigarette and the mechanic gave my uncle this rather strange solution: "You might be surprised, but it's good for your engine if you add a glass of vodka to the fuel tank every two or three days – it will help, I guarantee it!"

My uncle took his advice and…well, just picture the scene: midday in the square in Chernomorka. The local drunks are gathered in a circle, having a hair of the dog and putting the world to rights. At that moment, a man in a jeep stops near the alkies' watering hole and greets them as he gets out. He orders a coffee and a glass of vodka. When the vodka has been poured into the glass, the man takes a couple of steps towards the car, places the glass on the roof, opens the lid of the fuel tank and… glug … pours in the vodka, before the very eyes of the astonished rabble.

He closes the lid of the tank, takes his coffee in a plastic cup and gets in the car, saying: "See you all!" Then, holding the cup of coffee in one hand, he switches on the ignition with the other.

The engine lets out a satisfactory roar, the exhaust spews black smoke into the atmosphere, and the drunks swallow enviously. The car drives off...

That's exactly how it was – and my uncle drove that glorious mount of his for about four years before exchanging it for a later – and less thirsty – model.

Two

I once happened to travel from Kishinev to Odessa in the company of a chap called Sergei Surin. He must have been seventeen or eighteen years older than me, an officer in the Soviet navy – a commander.

He had served up in the North, somewhere in the Arctic Ocean, in a submarine. Then he completed his service in Baku and Astrakhan, in technical supplies. After the break-up of the Soviet Union, he moved to Moldova – I can't remember why. Maybe his wife was from those parts, but he was definitely from Krasnodar Krai; that, I remember.

Sergei turned out to be an interesting travel companion. He told me how Soviet spies used to examine the rubbish that American sailors had thrown overboard from their vessels into the Mediterranean Sea. Divers would find plastic bags on the seabed, held down with weights, and they would bring them aboard the Soviet vessel, where two trained colleagues would go through what they had found – and analyse it! There you have it, the other side of the life of a spy. They also have to dig through rubbish from time to time – not like in the movies, where they do nothing but hand over microchips and drive Aston Martins around the streets of London!

It was wintertime and, including the Customs inspections, the journey from the capital of Moldova to the Pearl by the Sea took about four hours – so he told me many stories, some of which I remember by heart.

For example, he told me about how the Israelis cheated the system during the Six-Day War with Egypt.

The Egyptian coast guard boats were fitted with missile systems, made in the USSR, which had a longer flight and strike range than the equivalent Israeli systems at that time. According to Sergei, the Israelis sent out a helicopter (or several helicopters?) towards the Egyptian boats keeping watch in the sea, flying at extremely low altitudes – basically, just above the water – and the Egyptian radars, picking up the movement, traced it and communicated it to the appropriate people. The Arab military decided that this movement was made by Israeli coast guard vessels, and they fired at them from their on-board missile launchers. After the enemy fire died down, the helicopters swooped upwards, and whether with the aid of some special decoy or by using some other cunning manoeuvre, they shook off the pursuit, leaving the Soviet-Egyptian presents to explode in vain.

Just then, the vessels of the Israeli Navy appeared on the scene, advancing on the enemy, and they struck, using their own weapon systems.

But there was another, even more interesting incident. Soviet submarines (among them, strategic nuclear submarines) were on duty in the region of Cuba, right under the nose of Uncle Sam.

Sergei recounted how Soviet submarines also kept watch around the islands of Reunion and Socotra, and in the port of Berbera, and other places around poor-and-friendly India and in the Antarctic territories…

But Cuba, of course, was a special case. The Freedom Island, and right next door – the Empire of Evil!

Anyway, to get back to the point – they had to change out the submarines every three or six months. They returned home, either to the Baltic or Murmansk/Archangel. From the warm Caribbean waters, they had to head North-East into less welcoming seas.

The Americans monitored the bearings of our fleet; no surprise there – you have the military might of the Soviets under your nose, how else are you supposed to react? It was important for them not only to know how many submarines had left the Cuban waters, but also how many were being sent to replace them to take over the watch, what type of vessels they were, and so on – in general, to control the balance of strength of the USSR in the region.

It so happens that between Iceland and Scotland (if I have remembered all this correctly), there was a cable laid along the seabed – a totally innocent cable in itself, to conduct some sort of intercontinental communications (apparently there was something similar between Iceland and North America). But there were special motion sensors attached to the innocent cable, and therefore all submarines that crossed this grid came into the field of the sensors and, consequently, their movements were known beyond the Ocean.

So, the Naval Command sent several vessels into the grid, sailing in single file. That is, each vessel followed its own route, from A to Z, and back again, from Z to A, at full speed and making the maximum amount of noise – it had to comb its grid in accordance with the "Top Secret" mission assigned to the captain.

Diesel submarines, some sort of vessels …well, torpedo carriers or something like that (I don't remember all the details), moving at full speed (and without crossing each other's paths), created enough activity and noise to be picked up by the enemy sensors; and meanwhile, going extremely slowly and often remaining unnoticed, a group of Soviet nuclear vessels passed through this region, considered dangerous by the Command, moving on towards the shores of Cuba to relieve the vessels that had departed from the white sands of Varadero and Castro's red dominion.

Naturally, in the best traditions of the fleet, onboard the vessel where Sergei was serving at the time of these missions there was a supply of very drinkable spirit – legal or otherwise, it had appeared there – which eased the hardships and deprivations of naval service. And so two or three weeks of these subterfuges at sea went by without glamour, helped along by numerous qualities and components, the most influential (after combat equipment and fuel) being: the high professionalism of the crew, discipline, fear of screwing up, alcohol and foul language.

Stress, mates – it sounds a bit like a winning combination at chess. They undoubtedly also boosted the noise levels in order to disorientate the damned Americans further, and the alcohol reduced the working stress – at least, that's how they justify it. As for discipline and professionalism, as they always say in the navy: "Drink won't drown your discipline!"

Later, when Sergei was permanently based in Moldova, he bought himself his first foreign car, funded partially by money he had earned in service. After a while he began to taxi people around – and he still does to this day. Well, and he likes to drink like a naval officer, albeit a former one, just like before – heavily.

Three

The third tale is about my old friend, Andrei. He served in the merchant navy – he was off travelling to foreign countries when I was still a second or third year student at the institute.

And so it happened that after one of his trips, he realised a long-cherished dream: he bought a car – a Toyota or Honda, a small passenger vehicle – second-hand. But this was back in the early 90s… everyone in the town knew that such-and-such a high-powered businessman had a black Mercedes, and such-and-such a gangster had a white Ford Scorpio; a foreign car was not only a means of transport, but also a luxury, the object of dreams and the envy of many in those days.

Once, in winter, Andrei was travelling along the Odessa-Reni highway, somewhere around Ismail. Winters are harsh here: ice and snow were piled shoulder high. The risk of coming to harm on the way was – and still is – great, and my friend was unlucky that time; he skidded off the road, and his Japanese wonder of technology was a write-off, wrapped around a post or a tree on the roadside. He wasn't hurt – he was alive and well, but totally stressed out and freezing cold.

This all took place somewhere near Tatarbunary. It was winter, the snow was fierce, drool turned to icicles in the freezing cold – he had to go somewhere and call for help. There was a small village about five kilometres from the spot where he had the accident. Ten houses or so – he didn't count. He wasn't in a fit state.

He knocked at the door of the first house he came to. He rang on the bell, a sheepdog barked loudly and fiercely, the snow swirled, and the wind burned his face. He waited, and the only thought in his head was where he could spend the night in the warm – to hell with the car!

The lady of the house came out, a sturdy country lass, followed by a man. The old boy was already grey (it turned out he was of Bulgarian blood); he was in a pullover, holding a gun, with a cunning look and a smile on his face. They listened to Andrei's story for a bit, standing on the doorstep – and then they let him into their abode.

First of all, Ivan, who was Natasha's husband and the owner of the house, said to him: "Sit down – you need to get warm." Saying this, he pulled out a vat of moonshine from under the kitchen table and poured Andrei a glass. "Go on, drink it – then Natasha will show you your room and you can rest. When you've had a rest, we'll have dinner." Andrei drank and felt the warmth begin to spread through his whole body, from top to toe… and happily, he managed to phone home to Odessa and tell his family, more or less coherently, what had happened.

He went to sleep and woke up around eight o'clock in the evening with Ivan shaking him by the shoulder. "Get up, or you'll get night and day mixed up. Let's go downstairs and chat."

So, they were back in the kitchen, but this time there was a hearty soup, boiled potatoes, lamb stew and… moonshine. And conversations about life, family, children…combinations of cigarettes, shots and snacks.

Seven days passed in this way: moonshine and heart-to-hearts became a feature of every mealtime – breakfast, lunch and dinner – until there was an opportunity to get away to Tatarbunary in Ivan's off-road Niva, and from there by bus to Odessa.

Andrei said: "I have never had such a wonderful accident, before or since. I left the wrecked car by the roadside until spring. Ivan towed it behind his fence by tractor so that it wouldn't be looted. I then went back and stayed with them for another three days – such warm-hearted people! Their children had grown up and gone away, and rarely came to visit – they really enjoyed having people to stay – then I came along, and that was their opportunity!"

Odessa
April-May 2017

MY FRIEND FROM BOMBAY

*"There must be a beginning of any great matter,
but the continuing unto the end until
it be thoroughly finished yields the true glory."*
(Francis Drake)

One

Morning seeks us out. Through the curtains at the windows and our closed eyelids, it taps into our consciousness, awakening it from its slumber, charging the blood with the timeless call to "Go forth and multiply!" And it is precisely that – not the need to get up for work or go to the toilet – which rouses us from our dreams. Why? It's hard to explain. Nature is just arranged that way; the species must survive and replenish its ranks. Some trees are for firewood, others are for growth. It has always been so, and I am sure that waking up to the world each day we discover it anew, pushing us to find someone in order to fulfil this prime objective of nature. But thanks to all the complexes we have burdened ourselves with ("Thou shalt not commit adultery," "Thou shalt not covet thy neighbour's wife," "career comes first" etc.), along with the distractions of football and boxing on TV, boozing, shopping and so on, the majority of civilised people can go through the day without doing the most important thing. And that is how civilisations perish – they become too…how can I put it…focused on aesthetics. On something shiny, perhaps even dazzling, and apparently much-needed – and meanwhile life presents an opportunity to the nomads and the Vandals, and they seize it.

And there you have it – the sacking of Rome.

How did I come to this conclusion? One summer, after a heavy night out, I fell asleep on a park bench. I was woken in the morning because my penis had filled with blood and was looking for satisfaction in the name of perpetuating the species – but I was totally unaware of my natural biological mission and thought it was just a call to relieve myself. I found a suitable tree, overgrown with rampant shrubbery, and, entering these refined beginnings of a wild forest, undid my flies, took out my "semiconductor", which was hot and full of desire, and spurted through it.

Some believe that because of this natural law, people who were sentenced to death on the gallows in times gone by would ejaculate at the moment of hanging. You see, for a brief time, just nanoseconds, their cervical vertebrae were still supporting the whole body, fighting for the life of the whole… before succumbing – irrevocably – to the law of gravity. But in those moments, realising that the body was on the verge of extinction, the brain signalled to its reproductive organs, and the penis shot out its sperm in a last attempt to impregnate at least something!

Apparently, it was believed that where such drops of sperm fell, a mandrake would grow, and the root of this plant would bring its owners luck in any type of shady business – not to mention passion in the bedroom – if they carried it around with them and never parted with it!

Once again, the drive for reproduction gives rise to legends. Can you imagine the Rockefellers or the Rothschilds dragging a root around with them… or King Solomon?!

Anyway, just as the flow began to slacken, and my cock stopped burning with the desire for sex, my eyes fell on a scrap of newspaper from which a lad was staring out at me. A little boy. The spitting image of myself as a child. He was just slightly darker than me – not African, more Indian – bright eyes, brimming with natural intelligence, and with my features exactly, right down to the mole on his cheek! I tucked my penis away and picked up the scrap of newspaper. It was an article about kids who live on their own in the slums of Mumbai, doing whatever they can to survive, while nearby, relatively close, Indian billionaires play golf and spend millions on flashy weddings for their children. In general terms, the newspaper was trying to highlight the contrast to the reader. Contrasts always draw attention, and attention takes up time – and time is money, as the well-known saying goes. And you know why? Because while you are reading all sorts of drivel about contrasts, others are earning money, and it is highly likely that this is money you could have been making yourself if you had been concentrating on survival – but you, your thoughts were filled with emotions, you were visualising the contrast in a country you know next to nothing about… you gave away (voluntarily, mind) your time and the opportunity to earn during this time, to someone else – well, for example, the owner of that newspaper – not to mention the money you invested in that piece of paper!

Unable to tear my eyes away from the photograph of that boy, that's when I came to this conclusion about our natural mission. Thoughts move rapidly, as everyone knows, and I remember my train of thoughts was as follows (if in broad terms I try to detail the main stages of the route):

1. Poverty, destitution, fear of death, instinct, will to survive, constant feeling of hunger;
2. Illicit business, criminality, serious crime, initial capital;
3. Development, awakened intellect, birth of children, creation of business model;
4. Attainment of sustainability in business, reinvestment, children growing up;
5. Purchase of expensive property, attempt to forget childhood, creation of a myth about yourself, justification of your wrongdoings, expensive whiskey and cocaine, mistresses, risk of divorce from wife;
6. Charity, speculation on the stock exchange, purchase of expensive and inessential things, children have grown up and want to move out, reconciliation with wife, withdrawal from particularly harmful habits, promotion of a healthy lifestyle;
7. Recognition in society as an extremely dangerous and successful man. Story in the press – boy who became a self-made man by following his own principles. Child (children) gets married. Long-distance communication, feeling of significant

loss. Back to the expensive whiskey, cocaine…doctors, heart problems, premonition of approaching death, lusting after younger women – and having them. Arguments with wife. Lies. Disdain for poor people begging on the streets as this is precisely where competition grows. These are the same Vandals whose task it was simply to survive. The task of the rich man is also to survive, but he is burdened with the load of legends, weak spots and responsibilities. The pauper is much more mobile and ready to commit audacious crimes in order to get rich. The rich man must consider his reputation, he is obliged to take advice from lawyers and advisors. This also takes time – his, the rich man's time. Which is ticking by. Someone younger and stronger, more aggressive will come along. The children don't come into it – they (his, the rich man's, former pauper's children) will never, ever have to struggle for survival. They won't be like their dad – they will be life's users, not doers.

8. Again, doctors. Intravenous drips at home. Strict diet and therefore feeling of hunger, relating back to childhood in the slums. Fighting for life. Weariness. Withdrawal from battle, secret consumption of expensive whiskey, phone calls to lovers, who contemptuously (and quite theatrically) sympathise and ask for money – money they will spend with their young partners. Emptiness. Death.

And that's where the chain ends. But then a new one starts. In this case, the young lovers were the Vandals, who destroyed the wealthy old pauper – for he wanted that which he had had before but could no longer manage, while they wanted it, could manage it, and took advantage.

The inner world of the man, who became insignificant because he had burnt himself out dealing in production and reproduction, was like Rome – formerly wealthy, but destroyed in the end. Or maybe the Vandals are, were and ever shall be money – always demanding love and reproduction, and destroying empires, then roving on to new territories?

You could say – yes, you could definitely say – that at that moment I discovered my twin. My twin-friend. But one step at a time, for you can't become friends straight away. For some time, I kept that scrap of newspaper with the photo of the boy – Vikram, he was called – in my pocket…yes, I carried it around with me like a mandrake root. But then I decided that this was some new form of dependency and I tried not to see him too often, face-to-face, so to speak. I hid the piece of paper in the pocket of a jacket I hardly ever wore. But the case took an interesting turn, as lawyers like to say! Vikram started to appear in my imagination, as if he were actually there in person; so our meetings and conversations were quite realistic!

But my twin did not pester me. He appeared on particular days, when I had already had a skinful, but my stomach demanded more, and my feet dragged my body into a bar. It was in the hubbub of the bar, with conversations (and sometimes revelations) being shouted over each other, that my twin Vikram visited me. That's exactly where and when it happened… Why my "twin" (as I said – he became a friend afterwards)? Because I understood that in spite of the ocean – or, more accurately, oceans – separating us, it felt as if we were very close. I was an old boy, who had made some money and drunk it away for no good reason. I suffered from gastritis, I had an enlarged liver and occasional bladder stones, but that didn't particularly bother me – I went for a check-up once a year and even drank some stupid pharmacological concoction, but then continued worshipping Bacchus, or rather, Pan.

He was a mystery boy, who was possibly (and I'm fairly sure he WAS) surviving in the jungles of Bombay and also making money, and would end up a hundred times richer than me, but at the moment lived on 3 dollars a day; and when he managed to pull off a deal, if he earned 20 bucks, it seemed like Moghul riches. And the thought that brought us so closely together, almost as if we were related, was this: "That could have been me!"

So that would seem to be it… but not quite – the most interesting part is yet to come! Since then, he has appeared to me when I'm drunk – or to be precise, when I've downed the first five shots at the bar and I'm feeling warm and light-headed. I order another and start getting too interested and involved in other people's conversations going on around me, and I get more and more tipsy, drifting off to God knows where, into a quagmire of memories and fantasies, where reality finally recedes, which is what I actually wanted. It's possible he is trying to protect me from alcohol abuse, but so far it is turning out to be the opposite. Sorry if I have been going on too much – it happens.

Two

"Life's too short to act otherwise," some great crime boss in Mexico, or God knows where, apparently said. And to some extent he was right.

I, for example, made money from good investments in other people's business. I wouldn't say it was child's play, more like a walk in the park on a sunny day with a beautiful girl on your arm.

I had a friend – now he's more of a business partner, but anyway – he worked in the research centre of a major fund, which invested other people's money in other people's projects. My friend gave me information and I invested the modest amount of money I had gained from the sale of my parents' house and plot of land in whatever he thought was the most lucrative deal. Money plus analysis… well, and a little bit of theft. That's the secret of success!

By fifty-five, which is the current age of depreciation of my body, I have accumulated sufficient wealth and I am no longer involved in the business. My friend runs it practically single-handedly. I trust him.

There was a change of management in the investment fund where he used to work, and which had been the source of reliable information, and then they started restructuring… in short, my friend was forced to burn his bridges. But, like the phoenix, he doesn't burn – or like shit, he doesn't sink – and that's good for business! He was headhunted by the fund's competitors – other paper jugglers – and he started to advise them. Big firms merely put on a show of discipline – behind the facade, there's a mine of information! They keep records of public statements by leaders, competitors and analysts in order to track any parallels. It is a modern form of Tarot card prediction – or, to be more accurate, prediction based on other people's opinions, which you can then turn to your own profit. As they say, it's always good to get someone else to do your dirty work!

So, you see, I paid with thirty years of blood, sweat and tears to achieve a good lifestyle at fifty-five.

As for family, I have a grown-up daughter, who lives and works overseas, and I also had a wife, who for a long time was a pain, and then, when I fell madly in love with her – she upped and died. I had a cat, too – which also left, and to hell with it.

Well, and Vikram, my friend and teacher. My companion and drinking partner. A damned kid with my face, someone from Mumbai, where I have never been, the land of elephants, spices and Kingfisher beer. And cows in the streets.

I had read a bit about Bombay, but alcohol and drugs had erased quite a lot from my head, and so I was left with a stereotyped image: dirty, noisy streets, with elephants giving tourist rides, cows defecating, adding to the filth and creating traffic jams, and street cafes where they boil and fry all sorts of hot and spicy stuff. And beer, of course – it's hot there!

An apocalyptic picture, especially if you stretch the elephants' legs, as Dali did, and add colour to the cows: something from the Hippy era, those LSD-motifs…rainbow-coloured cows with large intelligent eyes, in military helmets and with spliffs between permanently moving lips.

Beer-drinking tourists on elephants, like pirate captains on the bridge, are holding spyglasses, binoculars and iPhones, photographing everything in sight. The elephants trumpet, making a terrible din. Shopkeepers wave bunches of chilli peppers, encouraging you to try out some Asian cookery. Skyscrapers take your gaze upwards, to a sky without colour and without Paradise, for a world which contains all the things described here has no need of Paradise.

They have abolished it. It was an unnecessary investment of humanity, for eternal life doesn't impress anyone nowadays. In an age when Christians around the world celebrate Easter by sending each other stickers on Viber – ones with eggs and a cross and various other sorts of symbols – the idea of eternal life no longer strikes a chord in the hearts of the afflicted.

I mustn't digress into my reveries for too long, as I have a lot more to tell, but just take this one, seemingly simple example: does History, the mother of Science, really have to be so multi-faceted? Why is that? Well, the internet has played a part! You can find a thousand and one nights of History on the web, a hundred interpretations of one and the same event.

Where's the truth? Who the hell knows?!

One of my old acquaintances, a professional conman, set up a company which, by the way, is popular amongst the elite – he charges people extortionate amounts of money to create their family tree. Let's say you are the son of an autocrat, for example, or a prison warden. You have resources, connections, but you are still somehow not socially acceptable. You may go for a drink or a walk with university friends, but all the same there is a bitter aftertaste: "Hey, you know what? He's the son of that… son-of-a-bitch!"

The son of an autocrat came up to this acquaintance and ordered something supposedly founded on multilayer DNA analysis and meticulous study of the archives. To cut a long story short, the result was as follows: "son of an autocrat" is only the latest reincarnation of the aggrieved party, the one with the face of his terrible father. But he was previously a missionary, some time back in the 1600s, and he died for his faith, or from syphilis, in Africa.

He was also a royal personage – true, it was during the Norman conquest of Britain, or in the times of Khan Kotyan, but who is going to pay any attention to such minor details!

So, overall, his previous transformations were totally different from what he is today, and that means his blood contains more of the blood of all these glorious dead than that of his own biological father. And that's surely a good topic for discussion with his friends. An attempt to ride into their society on the wave of: "I'm just the same as you – and by the way, do you know whose blood is running through your veins?"

As I mentioned, the services of that company are in fairly high demand, but all it actually does is get specialists to gather online a number of seemingly ancient manuscripts, extracts from archive documents and other worthless bits of paper, all connected together by hyperlinks. And they show you, the client, something of this as the result of their work, because, after all, it's understood that the original documents couldn't be handed over…but their very good friends…and so on.

And then, as a finishing touch, they suggest: "Well, you can try searching for yourself now… now that you know who your ancestors were hundreds of years ago!"

You search and you find. As a layman, you little know that these documents were created by somebody, based on existing documents somewhere or other… Listen, everything is available on the internet, or nearly everything. You just need to know how to find it, airbrush it, tweak it a bit where necessary, and it will turn out like an authentic document. Well, what harm does it do? People pay money to find out that they are not really worthless pieces of shit!

Apparently, one man wanted to prove that he had Christ's DNA. Yes, he came up and said, "Since we all come from the same roots, from Adam and Eve, and bearing in mind all the interweaving that has gone on throughout history, I can assume that the Saviour's blood flows through my veins – I can sense it!"

They "worked on" him for six months or a year, and this was the approach they took: "We've got some good news and some bad news – which do you want first?"

He chose to hear the bad news first. It was this: "According to the analysed information, sourced from (and here they cited a vast number of books from the libraries of top universities around the world, documents obtained from specialist archives, classified material obtained by "our agents in Jerusalem and Malta"), the blood of Jesus Christ cannot be in your blood."

Then, after a short pause: "However, we have found that your blood contains the blood of… (and here he named one of the prophets from the Bible. I think it was Job)." How could he not be delighted! Not Christ, but Job!

It all became clear to the man, on the spot. "Yes, you see – I had a strange feeling that I was there, somewhere around!"

People go through many changes, let me tell you, as soon as they discover their connection to something legendary or holy!

And further, life follows its own course; nobody is a brother to anyone – or it would be more accurate to say: "All people are brothers, but money keeps us apart!"

Three

I open my eyes. It is an everyday scene around me – ceiling, balcony door (ajar), cats miaowing; and out on the street, grating voices – jibbering, jabbering, laughter, tears… I am at home. And she is standing, just standing there, asking me for something…I will never forget the look in her eyes. Full of tears and hurt, as if something terrible has happened. Some sort of fire…somewhere far away.

I sit naked on the bed, on the edge of the bed where I sleep every night. I rummage under the pillow for my mobile and scratch my balls with the other hand. I dial her number…

It rings. Far away, where she is! An ocean between us, a ring tone – a transatlantic ring tone. Someone picks up, for a split second I am still on tenterhooks. "Hello?" says a man's voice. It is a bit smarmy – evidently the latest boyfriend (it's about bloody time she made her mind up and married one of them…she keeps looking for "the one", but at this rate she'll end up with nothing!).

"Hi," I say. "Where's Anna?"

"Just a minute," the voice replies, with the same sweet and smarmy overtones. He is trying to suss me out, the rich father from across the Ocean! At last Anna takes the receiver and I hear her saying, "Thanks, Bernard," which means that this smarmy man is called Bernard – to be honest, I have never liked the French, but then I'm not the one who has to live with him!

"Hi, Dad, how are you? Sorry, it's been manic here and I forgot to phone – but everything's fine."

"I'm bloody glad to hear it!" I tell my daughter. Imagine what it's like for her. She is already thirty-two, not yet married, no children. She is proud and well-read. And she is always looking for something more – a maximalist, they would probably call it. She has some man with her, and quite possibly they were in the middle of a good old shag, and here I am speaking in a voice it is impossible not to hate. Intonation, don't you know…there is so much in the semi-tones – ask any bluesman.

"Dad, don't be mad at me. I'm a big girl, I can take care of myself. Everything's fine!"

Why is she talking about taking care of herself? What's wrong?

"Anna, what's wrong?" I ask point-blank. Emotionless as a rifle shot.

"Where did you get the idea that anything's wrong?! I'm here with Bernard, everything's great, and we're getting ready for a short break – we're packing!"

"Where to?" comes my next question.

"Agadir, Dad. It's in Morocco. We've got cheap flights, we found a wonderful hotel at a good price. By the ocean, sun, palm trees…what could be wrong with that?"

I reflect for a moment. From childhood she never liked flying, so maybe that's the reason for the stress. I remember my dream. It was a terrible dream. I have to say something to her. But I'm not sure I know what…I simply feel that I must stop her from going on this trip. Marrakesh is a shithole…

"Hey, so what happened to your last boyfriend, Sam?" I ask out of the blue. I don't even know, myself, why I asked it. I guess I just had to fill the overwhelming silence.

"Dad, it's a long story. Can I tell you some other time, eh?" I hear her reply. Her voice… God, how long it's been since I saw her in person. Just Skype, e-mail, occasional phone calls.

"Listen, Anna, there's a reason why I'm calling. I think it's better for you to come and see me. I'm not feeling too good, and I've had quite a few bad spells recently. Who knows how much longer I've got? Don't go off to your Casablanca, and I'll buy you and your Bernie some flights. Come and visit – please!"

It's an old trick, I thought. She won't fall for it!

She had a coughing fit. Then she burst into laughter, or rather, giggles. "How can I, Dad? I can't just drop everything. We've already…"

"Anna, have a word with your young man, or I'll talk to him. Listen, you said yourself that the tickets were cheap – and the hotel, too, apparently. I'll refund all your expenses. I need you here – please come, sweetheart. (I tried to make my voice sound as warmly paternal as possible, and not like normal!).

"So, what's the matter with you?" I hear her voice and my heart starts beating faster. I seem to have got through to her. What's the matter with me? I drink too much and I'm getting old. It's a lethal combination. What's the matter with me? Let me try and remember… "Acute aspirated mono pruritus," I say aloud.

"Whaaat?!! What the hell are you talking about, dad?" I hear her voice.

"It's not me, dear – it's the doctors who came up with it. Ok, I'm joking! My life has just become a bit suffocating. Too much alcohol, many consequences and nobody around to talk to, apart from Vikram, possibly."

"Hrmph!" (once again that irritated "Hrmph!" of hers), utter those female lips, somewhere at the other end of the line.

"Will you come? I really need to see you, sweetheart, it's important. You can come with Bernie, with Sam or whoever you like – a girlfriend, even – but I need you. I have to tell you something. There's a lot to tell you."

"OK, Dad – I need to discuss this now and call you back – give me 20 minutes, half an hour! I'll call you back." Her voice is gentle but firm. Good girl – I think she has listened to me. In the meantime, I'll go to the bar…it's just seven minutes' leisurely walk down the road. I need something to drink. Before her call.

Four

The bar, especially if there's a good barman, is like a second home. There's a TV. There's music. A toilet – of course. You can read a bit, pick your nose, be alone… To hell with that, though – I'm already alone! But all the same, there is something special about these rows of bottles and the bar, polished by people's elbows.

Do you know why people's gaze so often lingers on these bottles and on the bar, why we are so in awe of the barman's work?

My view is this: in the bottles we see our dreams, our past and our future. We see ourselves there, whichever way you look at it – we just don't recognise it. We think it is idle interest… there's a name, but what sort of a drink is it?! But idle interest and curiosity discovered the world, sent buccaneers away to sea, and caravans across deserts and mountains. These were expeditions following dreams, to find a better life.

Now, in the internet age, travelling has become expensive and is no longer so appealing.

What do you get out of travelling? You are a tourist – you are labelled. Or a businessman – another label, just a different colour. And both are targeted by taxi drivers, begging children and people selling hand-made artefacts, that nobody needs, from their arsenal of local souvenirs. Where's the joy in paying three times the normal price for a drink, let alone all the rest of it? Wandering around some site that was historically important in the 13th century. Castles, fortresses, churches.

Sorry, where's the relaxation?

There's no less history in your local bar. Here you can truly relax. And you can drink any time. You come to the bar, having slipped out of the office for lunch, or after work, on your way home; you meet up with people and everyone's got their own opinions… you have a drink with them, or drink alone. An hour goes by without you noticing, and your wife calls you on your mobile, shrieking accusations that her husband is an idiot and an alcoholic.

And what have you done? You only wanted to be a little closer to your dream, to have a little festivity. The smile of the waitress, who becomes younger and sweeter with every glass you knock back (why does this hardly ever happen with your wife?). A few words with the barman – he's a tough guy, he has a way with people and knows what they need…he should be president!

Isolated words, fragments of sentences, someone is being a dickhead, they're showing Rome on TV…how is this not an adventure? And without even leaving the bar!

The only inconvenience nowadays is that you have to go outside to smoke, but each to his own. I gave up smoking, so I don't give a damn. Everyone else could give up too, and then… that would herald a new financial crisis, as the tobacco companies are still monstrous.

They wouldn't repay the banks. The banks would start asking for a bailout from the government. The government would print extra money…but by that time there would be thousands of unemployed out on the streets. Agh…the death cycle!

"Once, a fishing boat sank at sea, somewhere not far from Thailand. Luckily, the fishermen weren't hurt, but they were scared to death. Well, the insurance company started looking into it, and they were told by the survivors, in unison: 'A huge cow fell out of the sky onto the boat!'

'Cow from the sky, my arse!' say the underwriters, 'That's not possible!'

They started to investigate. It turns out that the Russians were shipping live cattle of some rare breed in one of their large "AN" transport aircraft. They were for crossbreeding there, or maybe just for selling in Vietnam or Cambodia. One of the cows went beserk, and they resolved the problem by… opening the hatch and letting her go. Just imagine, for God's sake – a cow… falling from the sky! Bloody Russians, hahaha!!"

I picture the scene. I would have shat myself – which, I guess, is most likely what the fishermen did. What can you do with the Russians! That's how they always resolve their problems – kick somebody out into the middle of nowhere, that's their style. Then they have to hush it up – they are masters in the art of hushing things up.

Although, you must give credit where credit is due – it was an unconventional move. Maybe they were also frightened up there, and no instructions came through from head office. They had to sort it out for themselves.

I drink. The liquid goes into my mouth, my throat and flows further down – I can feel it in my chest…then bang, a small grenade explodes in my empty stomach.

I don't eat that much, I should tell you. I'm getting old – I don't get hungry. But I'm always ready for a drink.

He said "AN"… I think the head of aircraft engineering was called Antonsky or Anushkin. I read it somewhere. An, An, Anna.

My thoughts returned to my daughter. She'll call – for sure! She's your daughter, after all. Lighten up and let her make the right decision.

"Hello, mate," I hear a familiar voice.

"Hi," I answer.

"Bored again? How are you?" says Steve.

"I'm OK. Tired."

"Yes, you don't look too great. Had a few already?"

"All according to plan," I reply. "Just another day at the office. How are you?"

"I've got a new grandson," Steve laughs. "So I'm celebrating! Have one on me."

"What have they named him? Where is he?"

"They're in Canada, my son and his wife. They've got a baby son, my grandson. They've decided to call him Archie."

"Here's to Archie, grandpa!"

"To his good health!"

The barman is a middle-aged guy called Nicholas… he pours and winks, and smiles with us. This is his world, he is the boss here, and not some shitty client. Nick pours out two each…

"One for payment, the other is on the house. Here's to Archie – a long and happy life!"

I drink up and I envy Steve. He has a grandson, and my daughter hasn't even made a start yet.

She'll definitely phone…

"Eh, Steve?" I ask, looking for an affirmative answer to the question, 'She'll phone, yes?' or 'She'll phone, won't she?'

"Yes, probably," smiles old Steve. "What's it about?"

"Oh, just family business. Don't worry about it – you've got plenty enough of your own to worry about now!"

"I thought it was going to be a girl – I wanted a granddaughter – but when they said it was a boy, I was so happy I cried!"

"Cry your eyes out, Stevie – you've got good cause!"

I see myself from outside, as I move in the direction of the toilet. I need to relieve myself. My legs are heavy, I'm drunk. My thoughts are moving at the speed of light… Or at the speed of the stream… My phone vibrates in my pocket. I do up my flies. I look to see who called. Nobody. It's a message. It's from Anna. I open it. "Dad, we're going to Morocco. I'll call every day. I love you, please forgive me."

"We're going to Morocco."…it's as if someone is repeating this phrase over and over in my head. I had already taken anti-stress tablets, and somehow or other the edge is taken off my frustration. I simply feel heartbroken…

"I held you in my arms when you were a tiny bundle… such a little teddy-bear. And now time is against me. Oh, what are you harping on about – she's a grown woman and she might finally have found a husband. Who knows? Lead a quiet life, drink and sleep. What more do you want?!"

Voices filled the room. I stood at the bar again. Some young blonde brushed her breast against me as she walked past. Yes, those were happy days, back then! Why didn't Angela and I have a brood of children? Then somebody would definitely have come over.

"Nicholas, sir," I say, turning to the seller of dreams.

"What, Captain Obvious? You want another? Maybe it's time to call it a day?"

"No, it's OK. I want to drink to my wife – may she rest in peace. I just thought about her."

"Understood, Eugene. Your wish is my command."

He puts the glass in front of me and says, "Happy memories, old man. Cheer up! How's your daughter, Anna? Everything OK with her?"

I smile and answer, although there is a lump in my throat, "She's absolutely fine. She's off to Morocco with her boyfriend!"

"Good for her! Say hi from Nicholas when you hear from her."

I drink up. I'm allowed a little.

I look at the bottles. I hear a voice, a familiar voice. "Hello, Mr Eugene."

I see Vikram. "Well, I'll be damned, my little friend – where did you disappear to, young man!"

"I was working, Mr Eugene. I earned a lot today – selling paper tissues on the roadside. A rich man dropped his wallet and I handed it back to him. He opened it, counted the money and gave me twenty US dollars, so I did very well today."

"Yes, lad," I say. "I'm very pleased for you. Genuinely pleased. You can't get very far without money, can you?! Now you can eat your fill. The most important thing is don't drink whiskey."

Vikram smiles at me and replies, "I won't, mister. All the more for you. I've worked hard and I'm tired. Maybe you're also tired. Don't you want to go home now?"

"Hey, Euge, what's the matter – are you OK?" Nicholas' voice brings me back to the here and now.

"Yes, everything's OK. I'm going home. Anna is going to call," I mutter. "How much do I owe you?"

"You've already got two tabs lined up. Shall I add it all together? Eh, Euge? Do you hear me?"

"Yes, add it all up."

"Three hundred and seventeen, forty."

I take out a card. The money is transferred, and he gives me the receipt. I'm drunk, I walk home. Thank you, my country!

Five

I was woken by a phone call in the night – in fact, it was nearly morning. At first, I thought it was Angela's voice.

"Dad, it's me," says the pleasant – and now recognised – voice in the receiver. "How are you?"

"Apart from minor things, I'm OK. I was asleep. Has something happened?"

"Yes. Something strange…I don't really know. But anyway, I didn't go anywhere."

I settle myself on the bed so that the pillow is supporting my back.

"Hm… why, because of me (hoping to hear, "Yes, dad!")?

"No, dad. I'd already written to tell you that I was ashamed, but I was going to travel in any case. I had decided, and that was it. But as we were driving along, some little boy – he looked like a gypsy, dark-skinned and curly-haired – jumped out into the road after an orange. He had dropped the orange and… well, we hit him with our car.

"It wasn't the driver's fault, that's already been cleared. We called an ambulance straight away. They took him off. The police came to the scene of the accident – well, you know how they are…loads of questions…"

I sobered up rapidly as she was speaking. My heart was beating as if it had been filled with super-fuel and switched to full throttle.

"Were you frightened?"

"Yes. But the lad seemed to be OK. He was a bit bruised, but he'll live. I took his head and put it in my lap. And I stroked him until the ambulance arrived. He looked at me and said, 'You're beautiful. You'll have beautiful children.' I told him 'Shhhh – don't talk. The ambulance will soon be here to take you to hospital.'"

She gulped. It was evidently difficult for her to talk about it.

"Then he lay there quietly and took my hand in his. And he looked me in the eye. He had such dark, intelligent eyes. But he was a poor little soul – he was running after an orange. He was probably hungry. I fished out a 20 and slipped it into his fist. I said, 'Take this and treat yourself.' He didn't say anything, but then, just as the ambulance and police arrived, he said, 'Goodbye, beautiful lady. Tell him I'm fine and that I won't be coming any-more. He'll manage by himself.' God only knows what was going through my head at that point!"

I listened to her and the tears were rolling down my cheeks. "Well, I'll be damned!" I thought!

"Then we went back home. We talked for a bit…Bernard went out and got a bottle of wine. We drank it. Well, there was nothing we could do…it was upsetting, of course! It had ruined all our plans. Bernard tried to console me – he said not to worry, everything was OK. Maybe we could go and speak to the travel agent tomorrow and re-book for another day…"

"I'm glad you didn't go," I heard my voice say. The tears were still streaming from my eyes. I snivelled.

"Dad, he was our guardian angel. I probably wouldn't have phoned you…what was the point of waking you up, it could have waited till morning. But, then…I just can't believe it!"

"What?" I tensed up.

"An hour ago, we got a call from Morocco. They said there had been a fire at the hotel we were booked to stay in, and seven people had been badly injured…"

"What the f…?!" burst out of me. "Sorry, Anna, it's the shock."

"We would probably still have been on the plane, but it's really weird, isn't it?"

"You don't say – it was your lucky day! Thank God, you're alive and well."

"Yes, thank God."

She gulped again. "Then we called the hospital to find out how the boy was. It turns out he had run away – we'd wanted to go over and visit him. Such a great little kid." She started to cry.

I cried as well, but quickly wiped my eyes. I could hear Bernard comforting her.

"Sorry, dad. I just needed to hear your voice and I do want to come and see you."

"It's OK, sweetheart. Come whenever it suits you."

"All right… but I also wanted to tell you…you're going to have a grandson. I'm pregnant."

My heart leaped! I pictured old Steve in front of me the evening before… toasting his Archie. Now I would also have a boy! She said 'grandson'!

"Anna, I'm so happy for you. Congratulations to you both – I love you. Thank God, the Devil and the President – thank you all!"

Anna laughed. "You're always the same – you can't help taking God's name in vain."

"It's just my sense of humour! So, when am I going to see you?"

"Bernard said as soon as he can get tickets – the next available flight. We've decided not to go to Morocco, since there have been so many bad omens!"

"OK, sweetheart. Just let me know and I will tidy up the apartment. We'll arrange a big dinner in the restaurant to celebrate your arrival. We'll take a trip into the hills, to the vineyards. We'll walk by the sea. You've made my day, darling! You can't imagine how happy I am, I'm in pieces!"

"All right, dad… don't get carried away! I'll let you know our travel plans. Just hang on in there and don't drink too much. The baby will need his grandfather, so don't try to wriggle out of it."

"I'm ready for it. But in the meantime, I'll drink a toast. I have an excuse, and what a great one it is!"

"Well, OK – I'll call soon. Love you."

"Love you too."

I found a glass and some whiskey. I didn't often run out of these supplies, although they never lasted very long. I drank. To my future grandson. To life. To Angela. And to my little imaginary friend, who never came back into my world again. I wish them all the very best of everything.

Odessa – Kathmandu
April – May 2017

THE DEVIL, CAVIAR AND A VERY QUIET PLACE

It was a rustic house, the walls daubed with clay, with an attic that granny called her "garret" and several spacious rooms – and there was one particular room, at the far end. It was neither large nor small. It was in the right-hand corner if you stood facing the entrance, but that doesn't really matter now.

The house was cool in summer and warm, when heated, in winter.

Those were good times on the whole: the stars were large and so bright in the summer night sky, so close to the house, that it felt as if you could reach out and touch them if only you wanted to badly enough and stretched right up.

There were bats, crickets, water beetles (for a kilometre away there was a stagnant stream which flowed into the once-mighty river Tylihul), stag beetles and, in the wooden beams of the summer kitchen, cobwebs and cross spiders. I just loved all that wildlife! I would sometimes catch a fly and fling it into a web, and then I would watch the spider spin a cocoon around it.

As for lizards, water snakes, toads, hedgehogs…wow! You'll never see anything like that in the city – not to mention, of course, the cows, goats, sheep, roosters and hens. The kitchen garden, where you could play for days on end and feed yourself on the spot – an apple here, some raspberries there.

There was a cellar, then a bit further on, between the cherry and walnut trees, a few beehives.

The roof was slated, and beneath it, in the attic, there was a heap of old junk, including a huge stack of back issues of "Science and Life" magazine, which were fascinating to read when granny allowed you to climb up there. The wooden rafters of the attic housed several colonies of wasps in their paper-like nests.

When I had to fetch something from that far room, I was a bit scared of going in, I can tell you.

I was a little boy, full of curiosity, having read about Livingstone's travels and the novels of Jules Verne. The house was full of books – they held just as much of an attraction for me as playing games in the dirt outside. I would probably say it was more than just an attraction – I loved reading. I could read all day, and sometimes I even forgot to eat. I particularly loved reading about all sorts of travels.

I was a frail child – I was often ill in my childhood until I took up sport. And once, in that far room, I had a terrible fright. Just imagine it: I went into the room and there, in the middle, was a round table. It was covered in all sorts of stuff. There was an old newspaper there – "Pravda" or "Izvestiya" – what else could it have been in those days? Then suddenly the paper was lifted off the table by a draught. And from underneath it, I swear to God, the devil himself stared out at me, with horns and deep-set eyes and a big nose. This head was just sitting in the middle of the table and smiling at me. It didn't say a word – it was just looking and smiling. I was terrified. After that incident, I was even more reluctant to go into that far room.

Until I grew up a bit.

When I was about sixteen, I discovered that there was a collection of Soviet miniatures stored in the cupboard there – in hundred-gram bottles. There was everything you could imagine – Azerbaijani cognacs, Russian vodka, Moldavian wines, liqueurs from Tallin and herbal liqueurs from Riga. My late grandfather had collected them all.

And that devil was no longer my enemy. Not that he became my friend – I simply forgot all about him, about his very existence. I forgot my childhood fears, I wanted to try that vintage collection of alcohol. And now, sometimes I wonder: maybe at that point I began to commune with another devil, and the first one (which was obviously the product of my childish imagination) handed over to the next...

Either that, or the Holy Father led me into that room again and granted me the desire "to have a try" so that I would stop fearing the shadows of my childhood?

Or maybe my childhood fear protected my grandfather's collection from me, until the time was right to drink it?

Or the Lord gave me the opportunity to see the devil in my childhood so that I wouldn't fail to recognise him in the future?

And yes, in the future I did come across various devils, but they were generally actual people. Just like the angels I have been lucky enough to know.

That house has long since gone, as has my childhood. And I don't remember the taste of the contents of those bottles. But I was happy there – that, I remember well.

★★★

I once knew a man called "Baldy". That was his nickname. One day he summoned us small fry, lined us all up and said: "I've been hearing bad things around here. They say hucksters are trading on our patches, and our merchandise isn't selling well! You scum turn a blind eye because these hucksters are lining your pockets! Do you think we've gone daft in our old age? Or maybe we've got too fat, and our eyelids are so swollen that we can't see you trying to cover up your swindling? Boys, let me tell you something. We put the bread on your table – and by today's standards, you get butter to go on it, too. And now you want to spread caviar on top – at our expense?"

He had a point. It takes a thief to catch a thief. It struck home then. Of course we wanted caviar, as he rightly said. And we spread it on. But we tried to look sheepish and nodded understandingly. Thankfully, we remained in one piece – evidently Baldy was in a generous mood that day.

For he had come out alone to face the whole gang – true, he had brought an assault rifle and grenades with him, but his "guests" had hardly come armed just with catapults! He had marched ahead, under fire, and not sent his boys to the slaughter. There were very few like him, even back then. And nothing fazed him!

In business, he was a real pro – he was so good at explaining in simple terms what was what, how much things cost and who was the boss, that people were keen to make their payments on time and go along with him. He didn't take any extra and he provided jobs – but he showed no mercy to those who didn't want to pay up.

People appreciated that sort of man; even his boss – the top man in our town – greatly appreciated him. There was no nonsense with him – everyone knew Baldy was the best, if somewhat blunt in his communications.

And we, of course, respected him. You only had to mention his name (as in: "This is Baldy's patch"), and all those scavengers, planning to get something out of us, would immediately fall into line.

We didn't just respect Baldy – to be honest, we were afraid of him. But we wanted to live well, and that's why – one way or another – we carried on with our underhand dealings. We managed to make sure there was enough in the cash box and something to go in our pockets as well.

I believe this is what they call the art of management. Set up a process. Control it all in such a way that you don't miss a thing; don't upset the wrong people and make sure your hucksters understand that they must keep their mouths shut.

Each according to his abilities, as they say, and we were able lads! Even now we can turn our hands to various ventures, but there are many who are no longer with us. Baldy is dead, too. Somehow everything has turned around – and now those creeps are running the show. Bent cops.

It would have been all right if they simply fixed a charge or explained in layman's terms what you had to give them… and if they let people work for a living. But no, they stand their ground, telling the kids they've got to be honest, no stealing! Pay your taxes, keep your fingers out of the till and pay your gas and electric bills! Ah, and that leaves you just enough to go suck a walrus dick – it's a healthy alternative to food before bedtime!

Just look – these bastards want everyone around to be honest. And why, you ask? So that it's easier for them to steal amidst this circus. They've handed out a few crumbs and they've put on this show, a kind of reality show – let them be pissed on from a great height for that! And you can be sure that they pick the people's pockets while they are lapping it all up in delight.

This is how they make their business profitable, and they don't give a shit about the rest of us. It's exactly as Baldy said back then, may he rest in peace: "And you want caviar at our expense?"

★★★

"You know, this is one of the most peaceful places in town. You come here and all that noise and hubbub from the streets immediately ceases to exist. You feel as if you are in a museum or a theatre. You speak in a whisper. There's no rushing around." Our guide finished his cigarette and continued: "Then again, where is there to rush to? The cemetery?! Look, there's a grave from eighteen forty-something there… you can't read it anymore! These crosses are very old. It's quiet here, isn't it?"

We nodded in agreement. We were still suffering from the previous day's drinking and we needed a hair of the dog. We had brought some beer with us. The smoke from our cigarettes permeated this tranquillity, all these human stories written on the gravestones.

At this point our guide said: "We have one other quiet place in the town. It's really wonderful. The Armenian church, by the sea. It's quiet, you can go and spend the whole day there, sitting on a bench – and nobody will utter a word. We'll go there next time, shall we?"

We smiled and agreed amiably. Personally – I cannot speak for my girlfriend – I thought to myself: "It's good to know that there is still a quiet and peaceful place in this world that isn't a cemetery!"

THE REVENGE OF "SOYACAC"

I am the President. Many years ago I developed a formula which helped me to become President. It is an instant hot chocolate drink with added soya milk and is called "Soyacac" (from the words "soya" and "cacao"). A ridiculous name, isn't it! Well, I patented this shit and now I am President.

I am the President of a company, but I don't really need anything else. My company became the leading manufacturer of instant drink products in a certain Slavic country where I scarcely spend any time anymore.

I am now based in Europe; I spend my cash here and delight in the fact that so far "Soyacac" has not permeated its borders.

… I was a junior engineer despised by the senior management and I barely earned enough for cigarettes and as a result I was mad at the whole world but instead of hitting the bottle I decided to take revenge and I did this through "Soyacac" which is actually of some benefit to humans but only if it is made properly according to the recipe but if it is made the way they make it today it is no better for you than Coca-Cola and maybe even less so but people don't care about what they consume only what they listen to …

This idea again demonstrates what someone said about the information society, where everyone follows the trend rather than common sense, for very few people are able to think sensibly when they're being swept along on the flow of information. The rest have become slaves to the Word, from which, as we remember from the Scriptures, everything at some point began.

… but it is even more interesting that society today chooses its own figures of authority and it is not at all important for the person they call their leader to have done anything beneficial for society it is necessary for him to conform to that image of a leader to that

I got my break through a trader I knew back then who was award-
ed contracts by the army and navy as he had old friends in the military. As is often the way, he would always show his gratitude for
winning tenders by taking payment with one hand and slipping
something back to the servicemen with the other. But of course he
would keep the lion's share in his own soft, white, sweaty hands.

In order to keep the price down we had to sacrifice the quality, although we claimed that it was made exactly according to

the recipe, and then, when other manufacturers of similar compounds started to compete with us (because many people jumped on this bandwagon), we began to lobby our interests through parliament. At one point a procedure was approved by law under which trade organisations could not sell products unless they were certified by a scientific board for food additives and compounds under the government of our country. Strangely enough, there were many supporters of our product on the board, and it was granted all the necessary certification pretty quickly and easily, whereas our competitors constantly came up against obstacles and barriers. While our competitors dealt with these, we created new, improved modifications of our product and innocently came out triumphant, while all they could do was reformulate, rework and comply. As a result, they were burnt out, while our "Soyacac" became a national brand, a national product, a cheap and reliable source of Slavic Strength!

> *… life became damn good however we then started to be threatened from another quarter specifically by the authorities where a group of vultures had formed of people close to the president of the country who all tried to cut the ground from under our feet in order to make me give them a part and even the majority share of my business and they would give me their constant protection for as long as the system survived and our president prospered …*

But here I also proved myself to be steadfast, and I casually pointed out to the president of the country on the phone that ten per cent of the entire population of the country were currently employed in our network and we actually fuelled sixty-seven per cent of the inhabitants of this large republic with the compound and Slavic Strength (and these figures were supported by the results of popular surveys). I discreetly gave him the understanding that if, say, I started to run into difficulties, I might begin to shut down the operation and significantly reduce the output of production, and this would lead to unrest on the social level because I wouldn't keep it to myself, I would tell people the truth. The bitter truth about how my business was being stifled by those in power who were close to the big boss of the country – and who knew where that would end!

… but on the other hand if he left me in peace and allowed me to develop my business I could promise him since politics didn't actually interest me in the slightest that I would generally guarantee to support his candidature as best I could during elections and advertise his greatness through the medium of "Soyacac" adverts which would definitely draw the electorate to him and I would take care to ensure that the pre-election sales promotions of old "Soyacac" stock which was indistinguishable on the outside from the brand new product would be attributed to the account of our dear leader …

Bearing in mind the social status of my product, the national spirit and the health benefits which had been categorically proven by all the progressive medical professionals in our country, the leader (to avoid confusion, since I have already presented myself to you as the President, I will refer to my national counterpart in this way, going forward) and I came to the joint conclusion that it would be in everyone's best interests to leave me alone.

Because of my innate mistrust of politicians, and of ours in particular, I decided to leave the country for a while and settle right in the stronghold of hateful change – specifically, in one of the constitutional monarchies of Europe, cut off from the others by natural boundaries.

… I appointed as managing director the niece of our President who had just recently graduated from a very expensive university in that country I had moved to and in order to strengthen ties on the national level I managed to engineer the marriages of two of my nephews to daughters of the Minister of Information and Propaganda and the chief adviser to the Prime Minister on food safety issues which then enabled me to control the political processes in the country for I could whisper into certain ears and ensure

*that the necessary message was passed on through other people
and as I said earlier I am the President and in fact more than the
President for in that Slavic country where "Soyacac" operates I
now decide although not directly but through my trusted interme-
diaries and confidants fairly important matters related to foreign
and domestic policy and although this is of no interest to me it
works very well as a tool for achieving my aims ...*

Thanks to "Soyacac", the Internet, publicity and communications, I am quite content with my life, but as I have already mentioned, I decided to take revenge on my country back when I was
a despised junior engineer. In an interview with a well-known
European newspaper I said I was considering selling "Soyacac"
as a brand, along with all the production facilities and distribution network in that Slavic country of my birth.

And I named a potential buyer – a large transnational company owned by the descendants of monarchic families from the
country where I am now pleased to be an honorary citizen. This
same company is one of the world's leading suppliers of raw cacao powder and soya milk.

Straight after my announcement a major battle began, and
our leader personally berated me for my tactics, branding them
a betrayal of national interests! But since there was no alternative to "Soyacac", and our leader himself had helped me to remove any competition, I regarded all this commotion as nothing more than a charade and proposed that the leadership of the
country should accept my terms.

These were very simple: to oblige every citizen to take
"Soyacac" by law and to consult with me on all possible political and economic matters, and until I gave my advice (which
was to be strictly adhered to), not to do anything at all: not
to change, not to shoot, not to intimidate anything, anyone,
anyhow!

And, you know, the leader turned out to be a very clever
man and he agreed, but with the proviso that he could not force
everyone to take "Soyacac" without the threat of some form of

outside aggression, in the light and fear of which it would be necessary to cut wages to "almost zero" and introduce ration cards. These cards would entitle people to receive food allowances and "Soyacac" would be incorporated as part of the package. In this way, anyone who wanted to be fed under the state aid programme would be drinking "Soyacac".

A budget would be set up to pay for this, from which I would personally profit, continuing to send funds abroad – to the country from which I am now writing, whose monarchs were relatives of our former monarchs, though that was many years ago and wars also took place between these relatives on a large scale!

As for our plan, I didn't want a war, but understood that otherwise "Soyacac" would not become the rightful master of my country, and if you don't consolidate power, at some point you may be left totally without it, and that means without a livelihood, without the love of the nation!

Therefore, after the leader and I had calculated and deliberated it all, I was forced to agree to this reckless venture, although I was objectively in favour of a trade war, economic barriers and every kind of energy embargo; but our leader decided that it was necessary to "pluck the chicken" first territorially, and then roast it through on a low heat from all sides.

Strangely enough, our leader needed to do this because the state budget had long since been plundered by him and his officials, and in this way, on a wave of patriotism and battling against traitors, he seized and nationalised dozens of major banks and industrial giants, taking all their assets; he took control of huge agricultural conglomerates and either drove former bourgeois owners out of the country or put them in jail. He cut wages (as planned) and blamed the expelled and imprisoned capitalists for robbing the country's budget and also for spying for the intelligence services of enemy foreign countries! A state of economic emergency was declared, and there was a period of economic and political clean-up and – as the culmination of all this activity – a "purge"!

… they began to demand the repayment of foreign debts by various neighbouring countries which owed us money and when one of those countries began to resist and argue rather too boldly that they could refinance the debt with major international financiers and use this money to repay us and that it was international law and our demands were unlawful our leader announced a «purge» which implied of course that there would be war against that neighbouring country which was smaller and weaker than us …

Seizing part of its territory under surprise attacks, and accusing it of evil deeds, non-payment of debts and aggression towards the border population, which gravitated towards us culturally and architecturally, our troops entered into battle – although war had not yet formally been declared. As I have already mentioned, we called this a "purge", while our neighbours (with whose most influential and powerful representatives our leader had also stipulated the rules of conduct within the framework of this sacrifice), also somehow described it as "not war". Well, somehow or other they had to avoid declaring war from their side and setting a dangerous precedent for the hated outside world, which was constantly changing! We didn't write off their debt and they haven't paid us, so all territorial disputes can still be resolved in monetary terms!

We are waging a war which we can't win, for officially we are lying to the outside world that there is no war, but a "purge", and we are simply helping the peaceful border population to survive all the oppression and horror inflicted on them by the central power of the neighbouring country. We are helping them to clear their legitimate borderlands of any sort of evildoing. Within our country everyone knows that there is a war going on and they are prepared to see it through to victory. And although I feel sorry for our neighbours, I am even more sorry for myself – I have to support the leader because there is hardly any income and state rations will be stopped if we win the war!

The leader also understands this and I have retreated into the shadows – I am sitting here in Europe and happily looking on at all this from the outside. And to those of you who might now be criticising me, I defy you to try pulling off anything of the sort!

It is not our leader who rules the country today – and no, not even me. It is ruled by the crowd, the people (which is absurd in itself, because the people cannot rule; but our country is special – long years of experience have taught it that this is exactly how it should be!). The majority of people need my "Soyacac", because without that energy they no longer have any idea which way to turn; without "Soyacac" their stomachs and souls are hungry, and hunger, as we know, is no friend. So if you can get "Soyacac" for free, just by calling your neighbours evil and conducting a purge against them, then the people of our country are ready to accept such a scenario!

The people are submissive to our leader and agree with his arguments, but in fact they had always agreed with them, because, as I stated earlier, our leader is a reflection of the nation! All the people needed was an accessible and "beneficial" national narcotic, which I personally offered in the form of "Soyacac", and poverty and adrenalin only spur our people on to want it even more...

And the greatest thing is that "Soyacac" will remain in circulation for a long time to come, and I will continue to profit from this nefariousness throughout, regardless of whether our country wins or loses this terrible war for territory and power! It's a monstrous experiment, isn't it? But that's how it is – true revenge.

If they lose the war, I will sell everything to the transnational company I have been conducting secret negotiations with right from the instigation of the purge, and in private conversations I condemn the actions of our leader, who has already caused me to spend a year far away from my homeland in "forced exile", so to speak!

> *... I can tell you frankly that I tried this "Soyacac" once and although I quite liked the concoction I still believed that a good quality mineral water from the Alps and a fine Burgundy would be better for me but at that time I could only afford tap water and cheap vodka so I am not only gaining satisfaction from all this*

but also the means to pay for a good quiet civilised life such as I could never have dreamt of as a junior engineer way back then…

This is a perfect example of what people mean by "mixing business with pleasure". The Count of Monte Cristo was an absolute amateur compared to me, and what's more, I am a President.

All the events described here actually happened.

APPLES FROM THE OTHER SIDE

One: How I Didn't Emigrate to Canada

After my divorce from my first wife, I found myself getting more and more worked up about the whole damn rigmarole. I wanted to get away. It's never a simple matter just to drop everything and go wherever the road leads you. And my road led to Canada.

At that time (this was the mid-90s) there were quite a number of small companies in Odessa which provided emigration services. You only find this type of business in countries which have nothing to offer. I didn't see anything like that later in Switzerland or Britain, for example.

So, there I was, a young lad, fresh from university, turning up on the doorstep of one of these companies. I was greeted by a middle-aged woman, who conducted my first "audition".

We talked a bit in Russian, and then she suddenly switched to English – she was evidently testing me. She asked questions, I replied, and this went on for four minutes or so. She was delighted, because I did actually speak the language.

She called out: "Kolya, come here – there's a lad who speaks English!"

Her husband came over – or maybe it was her business partner, but he somehow seemed more like her husband. For a start, she called him Kolya, familiarly. I had a little chat with him in English. Then we reverted to Russian.

He asked: "Marina, what's his education?"

Marina replied that I had graduated from university with a degree in economics.

Kolya screwed up his face: "They don't need economists and accountants in Canada. They've got enough of their own. They want technicians and plumbers. But we do have an opportunity for you up in the northern territories – they are clearing the forest there. They pay well, and if you keep your nose clean, you can apply for residency later. We can help you – we know some lawyers."

I said I would definitely consider it. But the north was not really for me. I never went to prison in the Soviet Union, but for some reason I always associated the north with that kind of fate. I didn't move to Canada to cut down their native trees – I stayed in Odessa. It turns out you can also "cut the mustard" pretty well here – without any forests!

Two: Bengali Silence

We landed in Dhaka to pick up passengers on the way to Kathmandu. To say I was the worse for wear is putting it mildly. I had started knocking it back at the airport in Hong Kong, and it went downhill from there…

I slept it off a bit and woke with a splitting headache.

Sitting next to me, where there had previously been an empty seat, was a large, sweaty and very talkative Bangladeshi.

He tried to initiate contact with me, as they say in spy films, but I was in no mood to chat. I'm generally a sociable person, but not when I'm hungover and my head is throbbing, and without any background information.

But he was going on about how he trades in clothing and that it's a very good business. And he also trades in printing paper – and that's a very good business, too. And he also trades in spare parts for cars, tiles and other construction materials…

Then he asked me: "And what's your trade?"

Without a second thought, I said: "I don't work in trade. I'm in another line of business."

"Ah, I could tell you were a businessman – what sort of business?" asked the Bengali.

Just then they served tea with a shot of whiskey. I drank it and almost immediately wanted to go back to sleep. There were still several hours to go before we reached Kathmandu.

"I kill people for money," I said, drawing closer to the fat guy. "I'm Russian and I'm travelling to Nepal on business – you understand?"

The Bengali nodded to indicate that he understood only too well.

I wished him goodnight and closed my eyes. I didn't hear another peep out of him. Well, of course – I slept nearly all the way until we landed, and when we arrived my neighbour shot off ahead of me … he was evidently in a rush to sell his clothes and building materials. Business is such a cut-throat affair!

Three: Dance

Once, back in Soviet times, I dropped in to a restaurant with some friends. I can't remember where we got the money from – we must have made a bit on the side somewhere.

We were already in our thirties, but we weren't going to let that stop us – we had a thirst for life, so to speak. We were also thirsting for a drink – and then, as we knocked back a shot, I had a sudden flash of enlightenment!

Apart from us, there was also a group of gypsies in the room. Almost all of them were men, dressed in three-piece suits. There was just one female amongst them…

Oh, she was a vision of loveliness, I can tell you! Willowy, raven-haired, a tender voice and a look that cut like a knife.

And that knife pierced my heart. I carried on drinking with my mates, but my thoughts – oh, my thoughts were elsewhere…

In my childhood, I used to run down to a gypsy camp near our village. I learned to ride bareback there. It was great fun – total freedom! No schoolbooks or portraits of leaders.

But this gypsy was the girl of my dreams. She was gorgeous! She arched her brow majestically, and at the same time so alluringly, in an unspoken question: "What are you looking at, why are you sitting there… what do you want?"

And then – her smile. My God, I would have sold my country for that smile. And the neighbouring country too, come to that!

Well – if she smiled at me, that meant she was responding! The call of the heart, as they say.

I said to my mates: "I'm going to dance with her!"

The boys tried to talk me out of it. "Valera, they're gypsies, for God's sake – they'll knife you, then what are we going to do?"

"We're not going to do anything," I said.

I poured myself a vodka, went over to the table where the group was sitting and proposed a toast to the health of the men and the beautiful gem of a woman who had stunned me with her radiance, and I couldn't resist the desire to invite her for a dance. Just one…

And I pulled it off. I did dance with her!

How she moved in my arms. How her chest heaved. Her eyes and lips were so beautiful. She was sublime – that's the only way I can describe her.

It turned out that those gypsies were musicians and were celebrating the birthday of their elder. And she was apparently his daughter.

Anyway, I had an unforgettable dance – what a pity it ended at that!

Four: Apples from the Other Side

After military service, I began to hang out with street gangs. The Soviet Union had fallen, there was no work. There wasn't really anywhere to earn money in those days; I had been discharged from the air force and got dragged down into this quagmire.

There are so many tales I could tell. How my friend was shot by a guy with a double-barrelled shotgun and I couldn't get him to hospital in time – he bled to death in the car. I remember the look in his eyes – he was terrified. It was inconceivable he could die; he was as strong as an ox!

How we were once set up and ambushed…oh, they beat the hell out of us. Mind you, we had it coming. They almost finished us off that time, for some kid who had previously made a good living out of us.

My dad, a long-distance truck driver, looked at all this and said to me: "Igor, you're coming with me, son – you'll be heading for an early grave if you carry on like this."

Well, of course it was no bad thing – that gangland life had become too dangerous and drained away more money than it brought in. So, I gave it up: with some regret, of course, but I gave it up. I thought, "OK, I'll work on the truck for a bit, and I can go back to street crime later, if the worst comes to the worst."

I went all over the place with my dad. Russia, Byelorussia, Hungary, Poland – and even Italy! Who could have dreamed of such a life in those days?! I started to earn as much money as I could, and without spending it!

But my younger brother, Sasha, went down the gangland route. He was a kickboxer, fit and built like a tank. All he did was train, sleep and carry out his shady business. Mum was terribly worried, but what could she say to him? Two metres tall, he held a dumbell in his hand as if it were a shot glass!

Anyway, one day I rang home from Budapest and spoke to my mother. She told me that Sasha had not been home for three days. He had come in all beaten up – and I mean beaten to a pulp. He tended his wounds for three days, then he went off to meet his girlfriend, and the next day he was gone.

I decided at that point: "I'm coming back – I'll get the boy out of that shit. He can do some driving – there's enough work to go around!"

My father and I arrived home. There was no sight nor sound of Sasha. He had left the house and just disappeared without a trace.

We waited. We tried to get the police to help search for him, but they were no use at all! I asked around the local gangs, but was met with silence…nobody knew a thing. And, of course, everyone in the town knew him. We went around the prisons, the morgues – nothing. He had simply vanished.

Much later I met an old classmate of Sasha's in my hometown of Illichivsk. He came up to me and said: "Are you Igor?"

"Yes," I replied.

"You're Sasha's brother, right?"

"Yes," I confirmed.

"Listen, you're not going to believe this. I have no idea what's happening to me. I've dreamed about your brother the past three nights. He says to me in the dream, 'Find my brother Igor and tell him to stop looking for me. They buried me on the Ovidiopol road.'"

"No shit, so you have dreams! Thanks for letting me know!" was all that I could utter.

To be honest, I realised that this was most likely what had actually happened, but he'd come up with the details!

I went back to the street-gang thugs and told them I knew everything – that he'd been killed and buried.

One of them said: "Yes, Igor, it's true. Some big shots wanted to teach him a lesson, because he'd been giving them a rough time. But they went a bit too far – and he died from his injuries…"

I was bitterly upset, but I stopped looking for Sasha and whoever had finished him off. His fate had been predictable, for he was far from a saint himself – he was brutal with people, sometimes in the extreme.

Anyway, believe it or not, a month later I met that same classmate who had told me his dream about my brother. He ran straight up to me and said: "Igor, you're not going to believe this! Last night I had another dream about Sasha! He was walking towards me on a country road and he was carrying a basketful of apples. We met along the way, as there was no turning off that road, and he said to me: 'Here, take these apples – that's for doing me that favour. You told my brother.' He gave me the apples, along with the basket, and then just turned and went!"

Kathmandu, 20 May 2017

LEGEND OF THE FOUR BARONS

A demon does not testify against another demon,
a wolf does not eat wolf meat.
(Grigory Skovoroda)

One: War with the Genies

From East and West, from North and South, these legends crept into our world, hidden under the cover of yellowed pages. I bought them from Haggsey, an Irish sailor whose path crossed with mine in a London pub. I had to pay for the booze, so they didn't come cheap, because as we all know, an Irishman can drink the sea dry if an Englishman is paying! He had bought these scrolls from Ram Viswanathan in the south of India, who had swapped the manuscripts for tobacco with a nameless prisoner who was dying from leprosy in the Andaman Islands. According to him, he had won them in an argument with Tsen Yu, a dealer in antiquities and curiosities on the island of Formosa. Where Tsen Yu had got them from, nobody knows anymore, because apart from the fact that he was a Chinaman who sold secrets and all sorts of antiquities and valuables, few people today have any idea who this Tsen Yu actually was…

The world was ruled by four Barons. Three of them lived in the West and South, and one ruled in the East. The North was a closed country. Although merchants and adventurers strayed into these regions, none of them wanted to hang about for too long in the lands of the North, for only one law applied there – the one that was read out that particular day from the Wall of Laws. Therefore, the people there were confused and intimidated by the local lord and his soldiers. As a result, it became extremely difficult to trade and negotiate, for how can you maintain an agreement when one day they announce from the Wall of Laws that it is "approved" and the next, "rejected"!

So what can I tell you about the four Barons? They were men of brilliant intellect and great wisdom. Nobody knew their real names, they just used the following nicknames:

Va Ran – Baron of the East
Ti Ran – Baron of the West, beyond the Seven Seas
Bu Ran – Baron from the South of the World
Ur Ran – Baron from the West, between the rivers Danube and
Rhine

It is said that they were brothers, or somehow related to each other, but this could just be based on rumour. The mysterious lord of the Northern Kingdom was Ural, son of Goryn, known as "UsGor" for short. He was not one of the four, but as time will tell, he performed notable feats and that is why he will also feature greatly in this tale.

Once upon a time, disturbances started to break out around the world, and as they spread the Barons decided to join forces in order to battle against this danger. This is what actually happened: the Genies of the Deserts rebelled against other peoples and began to make incursions into neighbouring states. The Genies wanted the Barons to start taking their side and to align with them, maybe even become akin to them. The ancients used to say: "Don't bother to build a stairway to heaven. Set the devils free, jostle them around, direct them – and they will turn the world into such a place that the people will come and build a stairway themselves, when there is nowhere left to run!"

And the Genies actually were devils, set free by the people at some point in order to build or destroy something (exactly what, nobody remembers, for the objectives changed frequently, in line with the growing demands of the rulers). But the people and their Barons were unable to keep them fully under control, and then…what happened, happened! The story of how they appeared will be recounted below, and how they did not become devils immediately, but only later on.

Nevertheless, the wisdom and intelligence of the Barons prevailed in the struggle to survive, and as a result of this, many young people were sent off as soldiers to fight against the Genies. The war was waged across the whole world, and neither the Genies nor the Barons could secure ultimate victory. Extensive resources were spent on all this, and vast numbers of soldiers and officers from the Baron's troops fell victim, while many Genies also perished, as did ordinary folk.

When the Barons' forces were totally spent, they decided to arrange a meeting on Misty Island. At this meeting they decided to send messengers to UsGor to ask for his help in their struggle against the Genies.

The messengers were dispatched, but they returned empty-handed. Ural, son of Goryn, told the Barons that they should resolve their own problems and leave him out of it. He had no interest and saw no sense in getting himself embroiled in this war.

Then the Barons decided to trick him into joining the war against the Genies. Va Ran, who held several Genies captive, sent warriors from his "Dragons" division (the bravest and most fearless soldiers there ever were) to a few border villages in Ural's kingdom, where they slaughtered all the inhabitants and reduced the villages to ashes. Then he forced the Genies to perform the Death Dance, so that day turned into night from all the earth, ashes, dirt and human bodies being thrown into the air!

In those days any small child would have known that such trails of destruction were only ever left by Genies in the wake of incursions. News of these events reached Ural, son of Goryn, and his fury knew no bounds. The Genies had not faced a more bitter enemy since the time of the first Flood! The troops of the son of Goryn attacked the Genies in the heart of the Deserts, and the troops of the four Barons supported them on the outskirts. The Barons did not discuss with UsGor how to lead this war jointly to victory, but thanks to the information from their spies, the Barons often acted quite effectively and in collaboration, so that UsGor was unhindered on his path of destruction and went on to annihilate the Genies.

It would appear that all had gone according to plan, and victory was already in sight. However, Va Ran, who was not only clever and wise, but also extremely greedy (although undoubtedly far-sighted), decided to play his part. He sent one of the Genies he was holding captive with a message to their king – the great Jafar the Elusive himself.

You may well wonder why. According to one Eastern wisdom, when you look at world from the sun, everything appears light, but try glancing at the world from within the earth and you will realise that there is no less beauty and meaning in the shadows. Your eyes simply have to get used to the dark!

The Genies possessed knowledge that was not accessible to ordinary people or the wise Barons, and the cunning and wise Va Ran wanted to gain access to it, in order to study and master, to utilise and reap benefits. To this end he decided to invite the Elusive to see him, although of course in secret from the rest of the world!

Two: Secret Meeting

But wait, where on earth did these Barons and Genies come from? This is the eternal question, dear readers and listeners. The answer is not exactly straightforward, but the attentive ones among you will surely get the picture!

Once upon a time, a star fell from the sky to earth – and this was before people existed, such as they are today: heedless and stubborn, fearful of losing and not willing to wager "all or nothing", as the book of the Great Game demands, striving to elevate themselves at the expense of their own kind, forgetting about fundamental truths, seeking their moment of glory and then disappearing into oblivion!

So this star carried within it a tiny little box, probably made from star steel, or from the nucleus of a meteorite; in any case, from something that could not be crushed or melted down. The star burnt out once it had fallen to earth, but the box remained. Inside lay a message which was destined to be read by the chosen one…

When, many years later, the little box was opened by an uncommon shepherd, he found a tablet made of light material with the inscription "Play." Next to it lay a seashell-like object from outer space. It looked like what people today would call a nautilus shell.

The shepherd, who resembled a lion-like creature with wings, blew into this shell – and beautiful music rang out, reminiscent of the Universe. He had fulfilled the written instruction and played!

A ray from the Sun winked from above. The ocean, on whose shores the shepherd was standing at that moment, hissed with its waves, and out of those waves strode giants. People would later name them variously: Atlantans, Leviathans, Ispolini and dolphin-like Nommos.

These were the prototypes for these very Genies.

They possessed a huge number of positive attributes and a few shortcomings. To name but a few, their attributes included telepathy, prediction of the future, the ability to transform themselves, levitation, the ability to disappear and a momentary power over the forces of nature… Well, as you know, when thunder rumbles, rain and hail fall from the sky. Each of them possessed, and had perfectly mastered, his own favourite weapon: one a chain, one a club, one a hammer! And now it becomes clear where such characters as Thor and the one they named Zeus appeared from.

The shortcomings that clearly stood out included pride, the desire to dominate and enslave, and hunger for glory and victory at any price. Greed for victories…I would actually call it refusal to risk any chance of suffering defeat!

Later, enough of these few shortcomings spiralled into evils to make the creations born of the virgin waters of the Ocean become, at some point, reckless and egotistical in their actions and lose the strength of love and compassion endowed by the Ocean, which had existed in this world before the earth or sky or anything else.

The beings born of the Ocean initially came to earth to help the people – yes, yes, those little, unenlightened people – and to grant them knowledge. That is how a multitude of gods once appeared in the world of people!

And then came the Flood with its many victims. The people and these demi-gods wailed and only a few survived. The people and deities left to inhabit the earth and the underworld started to accuse each other over what had happened, and specifically the causes of the Flood. And this is how the words "devils" and "genies" came into the human vocabulary, in fact meaning one and the same thing; for the people's former protectors, their beloved gods, now became their irreconcilable enemies.

The people had to organise themselves for battle. All the people were united by one thing: the desire to submit themselves to the will of the strongest of their own kind, and not to be subjugated to the hated devils-and-genies! That is how the Barons and UsGor, the lord of the North, appeared.

The Genies possessed the gift of foresight and they could, as mentioned earlier, control the elements for a very brief period of time – everywhere except the Ocean; they could also transform themselves into whomever or whatever they wanted.

Va Ran thought to himself that if only he had such powers he would long ago have vanquished his counterparts, then absolute power over the people would have been his alone!

He surrounded himself with magicians and the most daredevil troops for safety (oh, how naïve he was back then) and met the chief Genie in his castle, situated high up in the Himalayan mountains. Picture the scene: a stone hall, simple furnishings, lamps burning. Va Ran is sitting on a humble woven mat in the centre of the room, in a circle formed by the depiction of two fish representing Yin and Yang. The Baron of the East is sitting on the light side. The Genie, who presents himself as a wanderer, with a burnt ruddy-brown face, dark watchful eyes, framed by a network of wrinkles, and curly black hair that is beginning to go grey, is opposite, on the dark side. They are busy with their conversation and playing a game of Go.

Va Ran, smiling, says to his companion: "I want to make you a proposal. Give me your ability to transform yourself and to control the elements, and I will protect you and your family from being killed. You can come and live in my land, in parts that the other Barons and your enemy Ural will never even know about. You'll be fine there!"

The Genie takes his turn. Smiling, he replies to Va Ran: "My honourable Va Ran, I can agree to your proposal, but you must listen to what I have to say. Otherwise, you won't get what you want."

The Baron of the East twitched his lips in response, faintly nodding his head in agreement. "Well go on, go on – I'm all ears!"

"There is a flower which will blossom in seventeen hours' time on the slope of the mountains which originate from the Northern territories, from the land where Ural, son of Goryn reigns. You must pick this flower on the first day it blooms and make tea from it. When you drink this tea you will die for a short time, and I will perform rites over you… When you awaken the next day, you will be able to transform yourself. The evolution of transformation takes several stages, and at the first stage you will be able to transform yourself into one of the elements, for example the wind. Into a gale, if you wish, or a light breeze, caressing the curls and skirts of young girls. As the wind you will undoubtedly be able to get into many places and discover the secrets of both your enemies and your friends. Then, once you have learned how to control yourself, you will move on to the next stage, and passing through that one, you will possess powers unknown even to me!"

Va Ran sat there in silence and looked, as if through a shroud, at the Genie. "Very interesting," he thought, "but what is the Genie going to ask for in exchange?"

The Genie read his thoughts and smiled: "Oh, Baron of the East! I want just one thing in return. Hide me away in a place where my powers will no longer work! Arrange with the lord of the waters for him to grant me a place in his kingdom and then the power of transformation will be yours!"

"And that's all?" softly asked Va Ran, who was beating the Genie at Go.

"That's all," replied the Genie. "I have no family, and according to an ancient prophecy my people will perish in any case at the hands of Ural and the Barons. And so now that I see that this will come to pass, I don't want to ask anything more of you in return."

Va Ran nodded in agreement and smiled. "You've lost, Elusive," he laughed. And indeed, Va Ran had won the game. When he glanced back at the Genie, he had already almost dissolved into the air. Vanishing, he said to Va Ran: "We have a deal. I will be here when you drink that tea!"

Va Ran sat deep in thought and realised: now he had to make a decision that would change his life for ever. A decision on which the fates and fortunes of the world would subsequently hinge. He was taking a risk, but he liked risks. Risk was intoxicating and made him feel young and strong. Risk offered him to sell his fear and buy power. Possibly, enormous power over the people and the Barons. Over everybody…

There is a proverb: "If you are tempted by love, give yourself up to temptation and fall in love; but if you are tempted by power, give up everything and run." Possibly Va Ran had not heard of it, and more than likely he had never had a love he could have given himself up to, apart from his love of power.

Va Ran smiled. He liked more and more what he was imagining to himself, and the idea of what would happen in seventeen hours' time and then on the following day. He was able to risk and to wager "all or nothing" because he was a Baron, and not an ordinary person.

He would have to negotiate with the Ocean, but he knew how to do that! In one of his prisons in the mountain caves he held one of the Ocean's nephews – a smuggler and pirate, known to the world in those days as Lam the Fearless. Va Ran would exchange him for a hiding place for the Genie, and whatever would be, would be.

Three: Initiation and Transformation

It must be said, dear readers, that people and even loftier embodiments of reason are truly dynamic if they see a clear goal ahead of them. But it is hard to be dynamic when you look the Ocean in the face, as you cannot see where its countenance starts and ends, and whether that is a smile flickering on its waves or a warning. When a person finds himself by the Ocean, either as a traveller or a beholder, all human activity boils down either to a struggle for life or to a peaceful enjoyment of life, depending on the circumstances.

However, all of us, one way or another, automatically accept the fact that the Ocean is deep and indifferent. The water is close and dangerous. In the midst of it all lies a thin strip of land, a small island: our consciousness, girded by the reefs of our perception. The ship that we call our soul often runs aground on the sandbanks and reefs of our perception, since our consciousness does not let it go further, into boundlessness and knowledge. "There might be great danger ahead," its voice seems to whisper. "Stay on the reefs, in blissful ignorance. Don't be in a rush to see things that I can't explain to you…!"

Va Ran was devoid of any conflict with his own consciousness; after all, his greed for power, the creativity of his crafty mind, constantly conjuring up new ideas about how his rule over this world would be more effective, and undoubtedly more beneficial for all concerned, once he obtained the secret knowledge – this greed could probably accommodate a very great deal. The phrase, "He could have drunk an Ocean of power," immediately springs to mind, but what do we know about the Ocean in order to cast such words about here, on these pages?

The Ocean, with which Va Ran had come to negotiate a refuge for the Elusive in exchange for the release of the Fearless… the Ocean sensed the presence of this strange person. Nobody knows what the Ocean thought…and does it have any thought process, such as we envisage these clusters of analysis and information, these communications of the mind? Do they come in a stream of unconsciousness, organised unconsciousness, like the Ocean itself? Or maybe it is just that when a person approaches the Ocean, he simply always gets what he asks for? So that, for example, just as someone approaching a pond sees his reflection, so someone approaching the Ocean with a plea, a request or even a proposal, automatically gets what he is asking for? The value of what is granted is not determined at the moment when someone's feverish brain requests it. It is determined much later, when there is a chance to look back at the attainment objectively.

And however well humankind and its great and strong play the game, the Ocean always ends up the winner, for it is an infallible player. The Ocean knows no yesterday or tomorrow – it is simply *always*.

And so Va Ran obtained the consent of the Ocean and, as promised, transferred the Fearless into the watery hands of his uncle.

Lam himself was to receive the Elusive in the agreed place, and we can all guess what Va Ran would receive in return, for the Genie would certainly keep his promise!

Seventeen hours passed from the moment of the last conversation between Va Ran and the Genie, and the time came to drink the tea. That very tea that would make the transformation in Va Ran's body, force him to die and afterwards appear in the world of the elements, with the ability to return to the world of men in his previous form.

The Genie was beside him when Va Ran drank the poison. The Elusive was calm, but deep inside he was celebrating, for now – once the transformation of Va Ran had taken place – he would be tied to him, to the world of Genies, forever, for they share particular characteristics: they are neither human, nor spirits. They are lords of the sand and riders of the elements, but in essence they are empty – as empty as the deserts. Deserts can certainly be beautiful, sometimes even stunning, but they are empty, for they once repelled the water and its power in the world, and for that they were punished.

The Elusive now found himself half-way to his dream – he was aligning the Barons with himself (and actually becoming akin to them, although they were not yet aware of this), and he himself was leaving the desert to make peace with the Great Water (this is what he called the Ocean, as the Genies were not allowed to utter his true name because of the eternal enmity between their homeland, the Desert, and the fullness of the waves of the Ocean).

Yes, yes… you read that correctly: Barons, in the plural, not just Va Ran. The Genie was cunning and had worked it so that… well, to sum it up, each of the Barons was power crazy, and each of them met the Genie and made a secret pact with him. Each promised to do "a little something" for him, as he requested. The Elusive, as we all know, could appear in different guises and in different places at the same time, which is what made the whole escapade possible. So when Va Ran thought that he was the only one in the whole world talking to the Elusive, his other three comrades-in-power believed exactly the same thing…as they spoke to the very same devil, who appeared to each of them that day.

One of the Barons promised to establish areas in the Desert where there would be no war, where the land would bring forth flowers and abundance, wealth and luxury for the desert inhabitants, although first and foremost for the human-like beings born of earth women and Genies, their descendants on Earth.

These places would contain vast amounts of water and vegetation and they would be given the name "Oasis", which would later become a common name in a world overcrowded with deserts, wastelands and abandoned places.

Another of the Barons swore that he would keep all knowledge of the Genies concealed from mankind. He would erase any memory of them and turn everything into myth, so that in the future, the people inhabiting the world would simply have to believe, for there would be no evidence left.

The third…

He asked the third Baron, in return for the art of transformation, to grant the descendants of the Genies preferential treatment in trade and exchange throughout the ages! In such a way that all the major transactions in the world would be made in particular establishments, whose founders and beneficiaries would be people desperately craving wealth and power.

So, in summary, what did the Elusive receive in exchange for knowledge and the art of transformation? He received: a hiding place in the Ocean, Oases in the Desert for those of his kinsmen who would unite with humans and form the Desert Tribe; concealment and distortion of the truth about Genies, and priority in trade and exchange for people from Desert Tribes around the world. As simple as that!

And what did the Barons and the people gain in return for all this…? We are about to find out – wait a little and all will become clear.

But we seem to have forgotten about Ural. Oh yes…the Genie also visited his Palace! Ural, son of Goryn, refused the Genie, for he was of a steely disposition and unmoved by promises. However, if you fail with the Tsar, you can succeed with his adviser! One of Ural's advisers was no fool, and apparently no less hungry for power than the Barons. And while Ural stood up to them, the adviser was ready to negotiate and share the world with the Four.

The Genie explained: he was to poison the Tsar with a drink, which would not kill him, but render him motionless for ever – the only thing that was required of the adviser was to take Ural's place in the Northern Kingdom. He would be silent and strong, he would be mighty, but without any further power over the people of his kingdom!

In exchange, the Genie asked the adviser to rule his kingdom in such a way that anyone seeking the truth about Ural and the Genies would be labelled enemies and slain, and those who could not be killed would either be driven overseas or brought onside so that they supported him and never again rebelled against his authority, being left in no doubt about it. He would have to ensure that the Law of the Wall always ruled in the Kingdom of the North, dividing the powerful and the powerless, and that the announcements made from the Wall of Laws were constantly changing. "Let this be the legacy of Ural, son of Goryn, and his reign; let it be called "tradition" and the "special way" of your country! You must do all this specifically so that the people in your Kingdom unwittingly get caught in the net of the Law and transgress it by committing unlawful acts. So that they become entrenched in this lawlessness and stop seeking the truth, looking only for ways in which to conceal their crimes, for if they start to seek the truth regardless, and find it, they will have no need of the Law, nor of a ruler!"

The adviser agreed to this, and on the day on which the Barons underwent their transformation and became demi-Genies, Ural drank the poison given to him by his best and most devoted adviser and fell asleep. Fell asleep, never to waken again!

At the end of that day, before sunset, all the Barons had first of all to become part of the elements, riders of the forces of Nature, just like the Genies who had suffered defeat and been beaten by the forces of Ural and the Barons. The Genies' blood was still soaking into the sand when the Barons died for the world in which they ruled, in order to be reborn, and exactly the same thing happened to Lord Ural, too.

But the transformation would not be complete in the mind of the Chief Genie without the so-called initiation! This was a special ritual, and the Elusive was a great authority on rituals.

So, what happened in the Barons' castles where the initiation took place? When they awoke 24 hours later, under the light of a full moon, sensing that they were reborn, full of unearthly energy and powers, yet also filled with earthly thoughts and desires, their first thought and their immediate desire was to try out their new powers – and they put this into action.

The following phenomena occurred in succession, at brief intervals, in different parts of the world:
- A volcanic eruption and very strong and destructive earthquake. This was Ti Ran testing his power over the element of Fire;
- A typhoon of destructive force swept across the lands of the East, terrifying the inhabitants of those lands! Va Ran danced for joy, testing the power given to him of the destructive East Wind;
- Bu Ran was granted powers the Lord of the South could only have dreamed of previously! He became the North Wind, bearing snowstorms, hail and cold that penetrated to the bone;

- Ur Ran gained the power to use the sun's rays, turning them into a formidable weapon, reducing all living things to ashes or bringing changes whose consequences could neither be explained nor foreseen for a long time to come.

The Barons were granted the right to use these powers only on the day before and the day after a full moon or a solar eclipse. That is why, from that time forward, the peoples of the earth have always spoken about full moons and eclipses in fearful whispers, as they bring changes which are by no means always pleasant or beneficial to them as humans!

At the moment of initiation, the Genie appeared before each of the Barons in the form of a beautiful woman. Each saw his own vision, his ideal, perfectly formed, a work of pure beauty. That woman, moving around each Baron, uttered words in a long-forgotten language spoken by the ancestors of the Genies who had emerged from the waters of the Ocean at the call of the shepherd and the sound of the shell from the stars.

The woman made seven circles around each of the Barons, and each of them was entranced. The blood, or whatever passed for blood in the bodies of the Barons after their transformation, seethed with excitement. The Barons were roused from their sleep and repose, they wanted to possess this beauty. It can be said for sure that the Barons fell in love with what they saw and wanted to own it, but it disappeared once the so-called initiation had taken place, and once again their elusive friend-and-enemy appeared before each of them in his usual form.

The Barons were overcome by a powerful feeling, probably the one that would later become known as passion. Passion, devouring everything in its path; passion from which there is no escape, like a curse, but which you have to live by and are forced to seek – and then, once you find it, it is impossible to drink your fill!

In bidding farewell, the Genie said to each of the Barons: "I have done what you wanted. You have become the master of new knowledge and now it is your turn to fulfil your promises to me. As for the woman who was here at the time of your initiation, your task from now onwards is to seek her and find her, and if this means having to fight against anyone whosoever on this Earth, don't shy away from pain and suffering. You will need the approval and favour of *your woman*, for only in alliance with her will you unlock the secret of the transition to higher levels of power!"

As for Ural, he was reincarnated as a huge mountain range, cloaked in dense forest and crammed with treasures in the depths of the earth, which is why, since that far-off time, his body has constantly been tortured by the people of his kingdom searching for answers, but forgetting their questions in their pursuit of treasure which their children and grandchildren will later fritter away.

Such was the fate of Tsar Ural: stern and unyielding, he stood up to Jafar the Elusive himself and won a number of battles against his forces, but ultimately he lost the war!

The new lord of the Northern Kingdom (the former adviser) gained power but was unable to hold onto it, for unlike the Barons, he remained mortal. As a result of his greed for power and the curse put on him by the Genie, he installed his family and friends in that land to ensure that they would rule and act exactly as he had been cursed to do. That's how it was, and how it has continued to be for many centuries.

As for Jafar the Elusive himself, Lam the Fearless led him to the secret place in the peace and calm of the Ocean. And there he would remain until he decided to rebel against the one who had given him shelter.

This would be much later, and nobody to this day knows how this confrontation ended, but I doubt that Jafar came out of it very well.

Only once did the Ocean ask Jafar to leave his hiding place to carry out one request (and it was for this very reason – because Jafar thought he would then constantly be made to fulfil requests for the Ocean – that he decided to rebel against the one who had given him shelter!).

One day, another star fell to Earth, marking the start of a New Age. A nymph, a spirit of the water, brought Jafar a nautilus-like seashell, and the Genie, emerging from his hiding place, sat down beside some fishermen hauling in their nets, and blew into the shell. The fishermen did not hear a sound apart from the normal breaking of the waves, for this sound was not for their ears. That music, that playing, was for Another, for the Stranger Who would later become the source of legends. And one of these would be about how He came up to the fishermen, walking on the waters of the Ocean as if they were solid ground, and began to teach them special wisdom and love for the One Who Sent Him.

"Wow, everything's so interconnected!" some reader will exclaim. Oh yes, more than you would ever think! But that's another story, whose ending has not yet been written. Every living being writes a little in this new book, but here's the problem: the Barons do their work – and everything that is written takes on new hues, it is distorted and edited by some people for others, and then again by those people for someone else…

And the four Barons, to this day consumed by their passions, shake and turn the world upside-down in search of their unique woman, searching for something they will never be able to find, searching for love in order to discover a super-power, not knowing what love actually is!

Apparently there is a proverb which goes: "If you spend too much time battling the devil, you will start to become him." The Barons knew only too well what this meant.

Ural was the only one of the masters of the world to avoid that terrible, all-consuming passion for a woman – a wine which the Barons still drink to this day and of which they will never have their fill. But he did also gain immortality and his share of love.

Ural hungered for the love of his people and he won it: nobody goes to visit him without feeling a love for those parts, and even those who drill and dig there, searching for untold wealth, are also filled with love – well, if not for Ural himself, then definitely for the treasures contained within his depths!

So there we have it, dear readers. Everyone got what he wanted. But what is the crux of this story? The crux was, is and will remain in that first message to mankind, sent in the little box from the meteorite. It was "Play", if anyone remembers! But who can tell us the rules of the Game? I'm afraid I can't help you there – you have to go out and find the answers for yourselves. But that's what life is all about, for it was said by the ancients that if you follow your heart you can find the answers to all life's questions!

The story of the Barons also teaches us that you may possess untold wealth and power, you may be able to transform yourself, you may achieve immortality... but if you are consumed by a passion that is driving you to distraction, yet you can't find love anywhere in the world, it is hardly happiness.

Odessa – London
October 2015 – January 2016

LIKE THE STARS

*"If only we could live with our eyes
constantly wide open – that would be wonderful"*
(M. K. Ciurlionis)

Episode One

Do you ever have moments when you want to send everything to hell and hide yourself away, somewhere on a patch of land where there are as few *homo sapiens* around as possible, giving off carbon dioxide and using up the oxygen and various products of civilisation?

Somewhere like the Tristan da Cunha islands, South Georgia island or, say, the sparsely populated atolls in the Pacific Ocean, or one of the small groups of archipelagos lost somewhere amidst the necklace of the Maldives or the cliffs of the Faroe Islands.

The appeal of islands lies in something I would call their "divine selection". Well, could these pieces of cliff or coral reef have been part of a continent? They could have been, but they are not, because they were chosen from above and trapped in the seas, like beetles pinned onto a piece of card. Dry land, encircled by the children of the Ocean's domain, as if by troops – but not surrendering to them! And in fact, it doesn't really matter whether there are any people on these lands amidst the water or not – although perhaps it is a little more interesting when there are people around! We'll see…

People are like islands. Well, it sometimes seems that way, although it is also clear that people wouldn't be who they are if they didn't communicate with each other. In that sense, we humans are always part of a whole. We are pawns in a great network which goes by the name of "*Socius*", and maybe it is that very "Word" (although this is mere conjecture by the author)

"

that prevents an individual from maintaining a discreet distance from the surrounding populace?!

In the city, you are forced into communicating – even if you don't get into conversation with your neighbours or your local shopkeeper, you exchange information by telephone or computer with people both known and unknown to you, and sometimes you might even talk to your TV – it can happen! And how often do you argue or agree in your imagination with "your own self"! In fact, you spend most of the day in constant communication.

On an island, you can try to become…like the island itself, or a part of it, and there is no need at all to enter into contact with other islanders, especially if you are alone there, the only member of the human race! If you so wish, you can choose not to look at the internet, not to answer your mobile and you can try to resist switching on the television, so as to avoid the news from the outside world. You are not obliged to communicate – you no longer have that anxious feeling that you are going to be late, that you are missing something… and all thanks to the absence of that damned information!

An island is an island – you might be there for a long time – slow down and try to enjoy what you've got. There is no reason to run, and nowhere to run to – but this is all apropos of nothing. Just to whet the appetite, as they say.

In some senses, an island is like a labour camp for the most dangerous criminals, even sometimes…hmm…a solitary confinement cell – and finding yourself there, you might become even more wrapped up in yourself, in your thoughts, because of the conditions! You are there now, and nobody is particularly going to miss you, hardly anyone will hear your screams and wailing – apart from the seagulls or kites, maybe?

But, without a doubt, there is something wonderful about this process of non-communication. You can catch a taste, like in the morning coffee adverts, of personal space – something you are utterly deprived of in the metropolis, a small town or even a village, on the mainland.

In a world where we exchange our allotted time for life, which we try to pass off as something special…in a world riddled with information about each other, in the seas and oceans of information, from time to time it is necessary simply to become an island. To be yourself – if one can use that expression.

And how about this for an idea: wouldn't it be truly wonderful, and extremely beneficial, for there to be a common holiday – three days off each year – for people the world over? No need to go to work, newspapers wouldn't print a single word, the TV would be dead, the power would be switched off, church bells wouldn't chime and mosques would remain silent…troops would lay down their weapons and go back to their families. Criminals would not go about their business on those days. Ideally, wine and music would be all that remained.

I also think it is highly desirable to take a break while you are still alive.

And here it is, the first break. *Dies diem docet.*

Episode Two

The picture came on…

A man was lying on the pebbles, next to a large rock covered in seaweed. Polyps, slime and foam, whipped like cream by the waves of the sea. A wet salty wail.

What might you call this scene if there were no ravens of the sea – seagulls or albatrosses –around? Well, maybe, "Solitude of the Castaway" or "Rock Face of Oblivion". The birds lent the picture a slightly different nuance – "Awaiting the Spoils", or "Before the Sabbath Feast", or then, unexpectedly, "Awakening in Torment" – because the man showed signs of life.

He was a middle-aged man of average height, without any notable features, although his features appeared to remain intact. His arms and legs, as he discovered, moaned, howled and whined in hundreds of voices – they hurt in every conceivable way, as did his whole body, although he didn't seem to have any broken bones. His brain seemed to be generating some sort of fragments of thoughts, for example, *"You bitch…"* (this was addressed to something, or more probably someone, of the female gender. Possibly to life, or death, or a seagull); *"Where am I?"* (this was a question to the surrounding space); *"I've drowned, I survived…"* (this was a conversation with himself, throwing light on the events of the past few hours) and so forth.

He couldn't avoid a loud expulsion of excess water from his body, which could be entitled: "Turning Grey and Throwing Up…"

Well, we have all seen something like this at some time or other, in a film about seafarers, or we have imagined it while reading Jules Verne or Jack London. This is not by chance, for the initial reactions of a rational man who has had a near-death experience are to try to come back to life, to non-death, in the quickest possible way. To the light. To home. To the community…

No, maybe I'm going too far – simply, any person, whoever he is, wants to stop himself from dying, at least for the time being. That excerpt could be called "Revival by the Water" or "Baptism and Transformation".

The man spent the next hour and a half, before the onset of darkness, trying to stand up. This scene is not particularly noteworthy, as he behaved like a small child – when he couldn't manage and fell onto the rock, he sobbed like a child whose mother has taken away his tablet (and as already mentioned, this was a middle-aged man).

Incidentally, regarding his clothing – the man was dressed in jeans, underpants, a knitted sweater, socks and canvas shoes. Everything was wet through – but I didn't want the reader to jump to the conclusion that I was about to describe characters from the distant past, like Greek heroes, who were more often than not either totally or half- naked, and half of them were downright sodomites.

No – this all took place in the present era. At some time not too far from now, about eight years before or hence. And, by the way, time rapidly loses its meaning when you are on a rock amidst the seas – all alone, like a hole in the backside.

The man found his niche (this line could have been an extract from the biography of some successful businessman, couldn't it?!) – it was cold and rocky but he could just about manage there – it gave him shelter from the wind, the previous and rightful owner of this place.

The man rubbed his hands and feet, trying to warm up and get his blood circulation going. He was still weak, and these movements, apart from causing him physical suffering, seemed like relentless toil. If there was ever truly a rock of Sisyphus, then this was it (as an alternative look at the classics): a man sits in the hollow of a large rock, which is itself part of the cliff in the Ocean. He rubs himself to warm himself up but cannot achieve the desired result. Hellish labour! Hopelessness.

Darkness entered his domain. The man became cold and frightened. He had not died at sea but now he thought he would freeze, and these thoughts, as you might imagine, were not exactly warming. He fell into hysteria once again. He looked at the stars and could not work out the Great Bear or the Dogs. He could not see any familiar stars in the sky, and this filled him with horror – thoughts were pounding in his head… "Maybe I am already dead – am I in Hell?"

Why is it that most people are wired in such a way that whenever they see something that falls outside their usual comfort, or semi-comfort, zone, it is immediately taken to be either a visitation from God or Hell?

But perhaps it is a chance to survive!? Maybe it is a chance to see your loved ones, children… who knows? In any case, they say you shouldn't give way to panic in such circumstances. You should say your prayers, get moving and do everything possible to keep up your hopes.

The man was unfamiliar with this doctrine. He peed straight into his already wet trousers and wiped snot away with his sleeve, which was heavy with salt seawater. His eyes were full of tears and he again gave vent to his emotions. His only audience were the seagulls, the waves and the crabs left in the crevices between the rocks. Well, let's call it a cheerful night following a successful day.

I am not being flippant – escaping death can surely be considered a great success!

Episode Three

How many thoughts flash through your head when you are hungry, and how calm it is – or visited by other thoughts – when you are full!

Our islander was not one of life's optimists, though you couldn't really call him a pessimist either. He belonged to that group of people who describe themselves as "not giving a shit". Or, to put it more politely, they tend to refer to themselves, without any intonation in their voices, as "regular, ordinary people."

Here are some of the thoughts of the man, who has had his fill of raw molluscs (probably mussels) and is feeling the warmth, as the morning is warmed by the sun from the East. He is also feeling drowsy, and has a headache and a temperature, which squeezes sweat from his body under the still damp clothing. The man also feels sick, and on top of that, he hears sounds from his stomach, which I would say were the warning signs of an impending upset.

Thought 1: "I abandoned Liz and my son. I betrayed them. What will it be like for the boy at school? People will say: "His father left him – that's bad". That's all people will say, and at first the kids will feel sorry for him, then they will tease him, and after that – it will all be forgotten. Life's a bitch – everything gets forgotten!"

Thought 13: "…if churches had a sign at the entrance – "Excessive Religion Seriously Damages Your Health", what do you think – would there be more wars and all kinds of crap in the world, or just the same?"

Thought 21: "Simon, my son. I love you very much. If I ever get back home, I will never abandon you. Forgive me, my boy!"

The last burst of conscious brain activity found its expression the moment before our Man-on-the-Island was plunged into the realm of dreams – in verse. Of course, it is no great masterpiece; however, in the catalogue of poems composed by people condemned to death, ravaged by the final stages of cancer or having been shipwrecked, cast away on an uninhabited island, without credit card, phone, wireless internet or other means of existence, this quatrain would be a worthy indication of how sober and self-contained the mind of a person still is, even in shock and stupor and awaiting the inevitable end…or a bout of diarrhoea.

They'll take me to the graveyard, when my time is up,
And then, long after that, they'll dig the graveyard up.
On this abandoned plot, a big house will be planned,
And living souls, in turn, will populate this land.

Episode Four

Eighteen months later

You are probably thinking that the Man-from-the-Island simply died there, in the middle of nowhere, and his wife is still waiting for him, crying her eyes out at her child's bedside.

No, you are wrong! The Man-from-the-Island grew stronger – as the saying goes, whatever doesn't kill you…well, you know, of course, what I am talking about.

He made an effort not to forget how to speak – he talked mainly to the Ocean, but sometimes he had conversations with the seagulls and occasionally held a dialogue with himself – deliberately using different intonations so that the performance sounded natural!

Sometimes he sang psalms – well, the few that he remembered – and spoke in all the languages he knew, as well as some he didn't – ones he invented on the spot.

He spoke with his family – his son, his wife (and incidentally, he advised her, during one of his conversations "across the Ocean", to marry a good man and forget about him…which is apparently what she did), with his brother and with his dead parents.

He also set about making the island more homely. When something was cast up on the shore, like a gift from civilisation, he would try to fashion something out of it, something he could use in his everyday life, to adapt it somehow for domestic use.

He learned how to catch fish using a rusty iron rod he had lifted up from the seabed, not far out. He sharpened it like a spear against a stone and sometimes he even managed to kill a bird with it.

Apart from that, he used a clump of fishing twine, which he untangled after it was washed up on the shore; a rock with a hole in it, instead of weights; and a hook which he made from his belt buckle – for fishing when he didn't want to (or couldn't) dive in after his catch.

But his main fare were molluscs and shellfish, torn away by his coarse, strong hands from the rock face and the seabed. This food gave him energy and an excess of sperm, and he would regularly use his hands, with some degree of pleasure, thinking back to former girlfriends.

His stomach adjusted to this raw diet – the Japanese eat virtually raw fish, after all, so why shouldn't non-Japanese resort to the same thing?! Water was a problem – but it rained fairly frequently, and he managed to stock up. For a container he used a stainless-steel tank which he had fished out as it drifted not far off in the Ocean, the day after his arrival on the island. And that's just when the first rain came.

The man spent quite a lot of time in the waters of the Ocean – swimming, diving, hunting for something he could make into a meal, and yes – simply for pleasure. Just think – no reprimands for skiving off work or penalties for being late!

When it got chilly, he would often do press-ups, squats, drag large rocks and work on his abs; he sheltered in his cave and warmed himself by huddling in a sealskin taken from a weak seal he had once killed when it was cast up on this patch of land. His "world-ly" clothes had turned to rags, and that sealskin was a godsend.

When it got warm, he sheltered in the shade of the cave, swam and sunbathed. He didn't have any books or films, but he liked to spend his time remembering films and books.

His thoughts moved from Hemmingway to Steinbeck, and he remembered, embellished, added and extracted. It was as if he was co-authoring in his imagination. To be honest, he did all sorts of things in his imagination, because he had more than enough time on his hands.

Episode Five

Once, and this happened very recently, when the man had been on the little island in the Ocean for almost three years, he saw an object drifting nearby, about fifty metres from that patch of land where he was living.

His brain did not immediately register what he had seen, but… that object was a boat. It had probably been wrenched off the side of some sort of vessel in a storm, or maybe an invisible hand (as per the theory of a certain well-known economist), tired of ma-nipulating the civilised markets, had for amusement nudged this boat towards this, as yet undiscovered, island market. A poten-tial market, of course, if you think in the extremely long term!

The Islander swam out to the boat, this gift from the Gods, and brought his floating craft ashore.

What a surprise it was!

Believing that he was located somewhere not too far from the mainland, it raised his hopes of being rescued – or of returning to civilisation, to be more precise. But the many years he had spent on the island had made the man's mind completely unfit to face civilisation. Both he and his mind had become savage. True, the Islander had not forgotten his native tongue, and he remembered that somewhere out there he had a wife and son.

But there he sat on the shore, stroking the hull of the boat as if it were his wife, as if he had been reunited with her already… and he was ready to make love with her, regardless of the fact that the weather had turned and a gusty wind was howling – fairly strong and, as always, promising changes.

The man looked distracted. He cried for a while and then laughed, grimaced and shook his fist at the sky. He hurled abuse into the emptiness, as if expecting that somebody would hear and start a dialogue with him any minute. He pulled faces at the sky, as if somebody could see his antics!

In the end, as darkness set in, the Man-from-the-Island slipped beneath the boat, curled up into a ball, like a baby in the womb, and fell into a sweet sleep, such as he had probably not slept for many years.

Episode Six

Aur said to Kingkh: "Come on, it's obvious what's happening here. Let's go and look at some others."

Kingkh was focussed on the picture, where the man was grappling with his own reason as to whether "to sail, or not to sail".

It should be explained that in the civilisation of the Sinnerags, which was hundreds of light years away from the habitation of humans, and somewhat more developed than terrestrial civilisation, there were public places for rest and relaxation.

One such place was the "Centre for the Study and Observation of Civilisations of the Universe". This was a bit like the Discovery Channel or TV wildlife programmes, to give an example of something earthly that most people can identify with.

However, the big difference was that, unlike the average human, who prefers to sit (or lounge) on a sofa or in an armchair, gazing at the images on a TV screen, the Sinnerags tended to turn up in person at the Centre and observe episodes from the lives of other beings, full of real-life thoughts and emotions, and they exchanged ideas and discussed various issues.

Moreover, the Sinnerags had never had a film industry, for they realised long ago that the imitation of life cannot compete with real life, so it was pointless to waste time watching films, theatrical productions, talk shows or programmes about the news or religious and political propaganda.

Well, just imagine observing all this: a man who has escaped death – a bit of "wreckage" from a sunken ship. His thoughts, which are focussed on other living beings associated with him, with his past, his… daily cares, if you like, his attempts to get through this. His emotions expressed in many shades, and sometimes in the form of verse. A "reality show", which is not restricted by the bounds of morality and censorship, and is not limited to life, but is quite often full of death, blood and brutality – well, everything which fills and glorifies the daily activities of humankind.

It is important to point out that these dramas were selected by a special expert committee, and on fairly strict terms. In the opinion of the experts, such live episodes should carry a specific lesson for the inhabitants of the local civilisation. After a certain time, the picture shows in this "museum" would be changed – and so it was extremely important for interested Sinnerags to come to the Centre regularly, so as not to miss significant details.

It should also be noted that, from the human perspective (had humans actually known about the existence of this civilisation!), the Sinnerags would have appeared as totally alien, monstrous creatures. They looked like a tangled mass of phosphorescent roots, growing from the top down and bearing some sort of resemblance to a plexus, crowned with something like an oval seal at the very top.

Well, like somebody dressed in a cloak with a hood… the face hidden, like those mythical beings you see on "Blind Guardian" album covers or in the film "The Lord of the Rings".

However, these creatures, the Sinnerags, have a high intellect and an even higher level of intuition, which has always placed them in the perfect position to make decisions.

Sensitivity and sensibility helped this civilisation to survive, because while humankind would ponder over a particular problem and resolve it through science and technology, and sometimes resort to the services of a holy inquisition or an atomic bomb, the Sinnerags would sense the situation and avoid the problems. They took the evolutionary processes under their own control and moved on to a higher level of the game of "life" or "survival", exclusively for the purposes of optimising resources and for the continuation of progressive and peaceful co-existence. That is evidently why there has never been a war on their planet.

Observation of less developed civilisations, particularly the human one, gave the Sinnerags food for thought about how not to behave, and inspired them, enriched them — for human civilisation was also, nevertheless, quite sensitive.

After humans, the next living beings which inspired them and gave them a mass of useful analogies were rats. Scenes from the life of rats often alternated with picture shows of humans, and the Sinnerags were sincerely puzzled as to why humans and rats hated each other so much, evidently finding the two species closely related.

The Man-from-the-Island was in the boat. In the morning the wind changed, the weather more or less calmed down, and he rowed with a piece of helicopter blade made into a makeshift paddle, following his instincts to who knows where, in the hope of coming across the mainland, any promised land, or at least of meeting a vessel on his way with living people on board.

It took him a long time to resolve to leave the island, having woken early, long before dawn. He ran around the rocks, he shouted abuse and profanities. He fell to his knees and asked for forgiveness, sang abusive psalms, twice went for a shit by the sea, threw stones into the water, shouted something incoherent — and his cry was savage, like that of a wild animal.

Aur had already moved on to the next picture show. This was probably a more entertaining drama — it was about how the people on Earth tried, with some success, to destroy each other using nuclear and bacteriological weapons; about who tried to save themselves and how, and how it all ended up. She preferred crowd scenes. The feelings of humans en masse…quintessential examples of suffering and heroism.

Kingkh stood and gazed at the Man-from-the-Island, who had left his home to follow a dream – or rather, on an impulse to rediscover his past! Quite possibly to follow an illusion.

Words began to flash up on the screen. These were verses which were suddenly created in the Ocean of emotions sweeping through the Man, the Ocean and Kingkh himself.

These verses were composed on the screen, scrolling up from the bottom… as the Man-in-the-Boat fiercely rowed in the open sea, while the weather began to turn again and the waves were no longer gentle, like kittens, but more like frightened lambs herded together, jolting the boat – "move, move… pshhhhh-hh, whooooo".

The Man-in-the-Boat sang a song… and the wind drowned its words.

The verses, born in the ether, drifted by on the screen, lending emotion to this tragedy.

Here are the verses –

Oh, boundless Ocean, dashing hopes
Of rescue on some distant shore.
Just water, infinitely deep,
Surrounds me – water, nothing more.

Why take this voyage with no aim,
Each heartbeat filled with fear and woe?
Each breath, which might just be my last,
Flies screeching from me, like a crow.

This wild screech, heard by me alone,
Begs, gnawing at my soul forlorn:
"Oh Lord, please don't abandon me!"
… But dreams are ended with the morn.

Awareness breaks out through my eyes,
Dawn's early rays have set it free;
Then melancholy quickly strikes,
On gazing out once more to sea.

Kingkh sighed – he seemed to empathise with this solitary soul.

The verses, composed somehow, by someone unknown, brought a tinge of sadness to the picture and, at the same time, a sort of joy for this madman. He would like to think that the man would reach dry land, but the picture was interrupted at this point. What was going to happen next?

These thoughts and feelings entered the consciousness of the being called Kingkh.

He moved along the gallery towards his friend Aur, who was concentrating on watching the destruction of the human race through the burnt offering of the planet, just like the ancient fire giant Surt coming out on the final day with his blazing sword.

"Don't you find this boring?" she asked Kingkh.

Kingkh replied: "Something suddenly struck me. Humans are so different from us, but even so…we don't have that…that quality."

"Which one?" asked Aur in surprise.

"That drive to sacrifice yourself for your ideas," said Kingkh. "People are ruled by an illusion and they are prepared to die in its name. Look – that man in the boat has created an illusion that he will reach the shore, not concerned in the slightest by the fact that he is actually far away from the nearest land! And it's not hard to work out, knowing the constellations of the stars in the sky or understanding the migration patterns of the fish which he caught for food year after year!

"These people – in this picture here – they have destroyed their home, their habitat, because they were motivated by an illusion… the illusion that it was *necessary* to do this in order to find happiness. But it is not difficult to understand that this path destroys *all* life, and that moreover it takes enormous evolutionary efforts to generate the rational sequence of events – and create new life!"

"Yes," said Aur. "The need to destroy each other is the distinguishing feature of their civilisation. But it is interesting that, at the same time, they are quite sensitive, and they aim for the stars, for infinity, immortality. They believe this is the ideal solution to all their troubles, but since there is no way they will ever achieve their aim, they carry on accusing and destroying each other, looking everywhere for someone else to blame.

"But we've watched enough of this now. Let's go and look at the stars. There's no reason to get all worked up – I'm tired of it. It's time to be a little unfeeling for a while … like the stars themselves."

November 2016–January 14, 2017
Odessa – Lvov

FLOWERS OF DARKNESS

One

The door was adorned with a silver plaque, which read "*Post Factum Management*" but offered no further information.

The office was austere, decorated in classical dark purple and brown tones, with marble, expensive Chinese porcelain and silver. Samael Iblis, the boss of all bosses, sat solemnly in the darkness of the office and thoughtfully turned over his rosary, waiting for one of the most influential people in the city – or arguably the entire world – to arrive.

The esteemed gentleman, by the name of Geoff Ironson, was due to appear any minute to discuss a somewhat delicate matter.

What can be said about Mr Ironson? The newspapers reported that he was a self-made man, who started out working for a courier service and was scarcely able to make ends meet. He was then spotted by one of the semi-criminal dealers in the Latin Quarter, a man known as Giovanni Qbira, and started to work for his firm, which was used to place bets on sweepstakes and to bid in tenders announced by certain municipal bodies. In other words, he stole taxpayers' money with the help of his connections in the mafia and the civil service and invested it in betting on sporting events. He was surprisingly lucky.

He bet on everything from horseracing to boxing, from cock-fighting (such a favourite of the Filipino community) to baseball and sailing regattas.

As already mentioned, Don Qbira was a man with connections – and the young Mr Ironson very soon learned and understood how real, non-office business operated. Insider dealing, as it is called nowadays – contemptible on the one hand, and yet the source of excitement to so many. Sun Tzu wrote in his treatise on war that reliable information about the enemy's plans is not brought by angels or demons but obtained from spies. And what is business, if not war?!

Mr Ironson became an adviser to Mr Qbira, and when he died – or rather, disappeared without trace during his latest trip to Malta – Geoff, with the approval of the remaining members of the family, began to manage the affairs of the late Don Giovanni in the interests of his two daughters and widow (who did not grieve for too long and soon found herself a new "catch").

The company which Ironson managed started to invest the profits from successful bets in shares, bonds, futures and options, and to purchase property. It soon expanded to the size of a transnational conglomerate, active in the sphere of international shipping and the financial and banking sectors. One of the corporation's prize acquisitions was a certain European bank, renowned for its 150-year history, which Geoff bought for a comparatively small sum, as the business was on the verge of bankruptcy.

And, of course, there was betting…

Apart from sporting bets, Geoff played for high stakes on international financial markets – he speculated on shares, futures and other securities, and after going through a series of ups and downs, he finally reached Olympus; the "Ai-Qbira International" group of companies was recently estimated to be worth thirteen billion dollars, which you will agree is no small sum!

Mr Ironson had a family – a wife and young son, and a brother in California, but nobody else. However, this was compensated by the thousands of people with whom Geoff communicated on business matters every God-given day. As they say, "My burden is my blessing."

But there was one thing which prevented Mr Ironson from being at peace with the world, despite the fact he must have been rolling in money! He was not accepted as an equal by certain circles in society – these "certain circles" being a particular ancient order originating in Malta, where Don Qbira hailed from, God rest his sinful soul!

Geoff sent them letters, but they were returned marked "Not known at this address". He tried to find some "leads"…he was beside himself with excitement, but met with no response! Yet he felt sure that what he was looking for, this thing gnawing at his consciousness day and night – or rather, this knowledge – was to be found right there, in the possession of that ancient order. This feeling nagged at him relentlessly – and finally led him to Post Factum.

What could a businessman like S. Iblis do for Mr Ironson? What did he deal in?

Mr Iblis and his company, *Post Factum Management*, dealt with particularly important clients, tracing the roots from their distant past and, correspondingly, their family connections. This enabled former gangsters or paper boys, who had got rich quick on whatever it was they did to make money, to transform themselves into the high-born descendants of ancient noble families, knights, monarchs, pioneers and scientists.

As opposed to other companies, which could trace DNA to seek the roots of the nouveau riche in central Africa or Afghanistan, for example, Post Factum Management would start by finding out what the client particularly wanted, who he would like to be, what type of blueblood he would like to be related to…

A question Mr Iblis frequently asked was: "Imagine that you have died. Apart from the money passed onto your heirs, what mark will be left in history? What would you like to see there, after you've gone, what sort of records, what legacy?"

This was a question that left many of his clients stumped. Could you really choose your own lineage? This was definitely beginning to sound a bit dubious!

But Mr Iblis had a ready answer. He put forward arguments that convinced many of them, if not all. In the beginning there were two people, right? You've read about it! Well, if we are genetically related to those two people, from whom all others are descended, then it's just a case of meticulous checking and analysis. Well, you can spend years on this, and in practice, such intergeneric bridges have taken from seven months to two and a half years to identify.

Of course, everything was backed by supporting evidence – scientific proof, nothing speculative. There were sometimes also historical notes, archive records and other documents which, directly or indirectly, confirmed ancestry. Sometimes, on the contrary, it was necessary to find evidence that a person had never been related to someone or other. For example, you are the son of a dictator – let's say Pinochet, or someone like that – nowadays, as ever, there are plenty of them about!

You can adopt your wife's surname, but you know those meddling journalists – they'll dig it up and drag it out into the open.

Mr Iblis would prove, quite objectively – once again using the very best technology – that a person who has the blood of a dictator flowing through his veins has far more "good" blood inside him, if you consider all the distinguished kinsmen over the past, say, 500 or 800 years. By simply labelling a person as the son of a murderous dictator, journalists and opponents are committing a crime against history, for in the end, it turns out that he is also the great-great-great grandson of some hidalgo, or he's related to a European monarch! Who knows what might have transpired over hundreds and hundreds of years of history.

Post Factum Management prided itself on its status and reputation! And reputation in the world of wealth is a mighty asset. The company did not advertise. Iblis did not go to forums in Davos or academic conferences. He preferred selective contacts and information which you couldn't get from the morning papers or see on the screen when you switched on your computer. In this regard his approach to business was very similar to Geoff Ironson's, and he had a feeling that their conversation would mark the start of a good deal.

Two

"You are probably familiar with this Order, Mr Iblis," began Mr Ironson, smiling and getting straight down to business. "'The Renunciates' is one of those Orders which, like Nepal or Japan some centuries ago, does not admit any outsiders. As far as I know on this matter – and I know a fair amount – they possess very valuable information about the true role of Jesus and about the precursors to what we now call Christianity. I'm sure you'll agree that it's not a case of mass insanity – it's a code. A code which can be used to control millions of people on the planet. And some small group of people – they may be extremely worthy, but all the same, they're just people – possess information which could help to unlock this code for humanity, but they won't let anyone into their circle. I want to change that. Are you able to help me find someone amongst my ancestors, virtual or actual, who would have had a connection with this group?"

Deep in thought, Mr Iblis looked like the hero of some grand opera. His eyes shone with intellect and pride. This combination was common to his distinguished ancestor, if you can put it like that – for you see, we are all to some extent just the parallel transfer of our genetic data from one point in space to another, to use mathematical terms.

He was certainly able to help, and he knew it. But his nature was, and still is, such that he always tries to think a game of chess through to the end and he always – oh yes, without exception – plays to win.

Is chess too dull for you? Then take good old poker. Yes, his moves were closer to this card game, as some element of bluff was intrinsic to the way in which he conducted his business. But nobody is whiter than white – he knew that better than anyone! You could expand on this ad infinitum, but we don't have that much time – for everyone has his own business to attend to, and who knows what might happen tomorrow? Therefore, the narrator is going to cut some of the dialogue and thoughts of the characters, but only a little…just so that the central idea of the story does not go adrift or become hidden behind a screen of mundane idioms.

The conversation continued. S. Iblis put on an air of concentration and made notes in his notebook. Mr Ironson was bursting with impatience but remained outwardly calm, and even indifferent, portraying a sort of indolence, and from time to time glancing at his Swiss Vacheron Constantin chronometer watch, as if letting his companion know that his time was a pretty valuable asset.

S. Iblis made out that he had not noticed this vulgarity, although he was secretly enjoying it. He had come across different character types over his career, and this "man-shell", as he called people like Ironson, according to his own classification, was nothing new to his collection.

Why "shell"? Well, it's the shape – a fairly wide opening and many layers, twists and turns, all alike, aiming towards the cone, the final spiral, to refinement. At the same time, there is no exit – or rather, it is back in the same place as the entrance. And inside it contains a pleasant noise, incomparable to anything else; well, you know, of course, that if you hold a shell to your ear, you hear a noise. Sailors say that it is the wind and the sea arguing with each other, medicine affirms that this noise is caused by the flow of blood through the arteries of the head, but Mr Iblis had no theory on the matter. Noise is noise…

Three

S. Iblis did not accompany Mr Ironson to Malta. He was tied up with a trip to San Francisco, so he gave Geoff free rein – and of course, provided access to his contacts and useful information.

Having grown as a businessman amongst Maltese immigrants in America, Geoff asked for assistance from the family of his former employer. Qbira's successors were pleased to help.

It should probably be pointed out that Mr Ironson did not mention this to Mr Iblis, despite their agreement on total openness

in this venture. It is not clear why he decided to keep it quiet…
it might simply have been intuition.

Amidst the mediaeval and more contemporary architecture
of Valetta, amidst the narrow back streets, the restaurants serving
seafood, which Mr Ironson was so partial to, and the hospitality of
Don Qbira's descendants, the first two days of the trip passed by.

Geoff was not given to emotion, but he liked the atmosphere –
the aura of secret and ancient knowledge which was locked away
somewhere here, behind the yellow-brown walls, in books and
manuscripts, combined with the utterly modern desire to compete, make money and spend it.

He had one meeting over the course of those days, with a
"mate of S. Iblis" – as the maestro himself put it. The "mate"
turned out to be a lady-lawyer, Adele de Maria, but apart from
the fact that she was a professional in the field of modern company law, she was also considered an expert in Roman law and
an authority on religious movements and Orders, of which there
have always been a good many, some even based on Malta's rugged
shores. The most famous is of course the Order of Hospitallers.
The least well-known, and possibly the least researched and most
closed Order, is that of the Renunciates.

Adele de Maria did not give Geoffrey any substantially new information, but she promised to help. She said that she would need
to talk it all over with Mr Iblis, but the only course that seemed
reasonable to her, considering the time factor, was, frankly speaking, to use a spy to find a way to communicate with the Order.

Mr Ironson only had just over two days left to make contact
with a representative of the Order, and as a senior manager in
business, he wanted to speak to someone on a similar level. He
seemed to have reached a dead-end: S. Iblis had not yet presented
him with any information about his "kinship" with the Order,
though he kept assuring him on the phone that work was un-
derway and that connections would be established any day now!

The lady-lawyer stated quite plainly that she would have to
use all her contacts, right down to the mafia-style cells on the island, to gain access to the Order, for all legal approaches seemed

blocked and futile. Qbira's descendants smiled and invited him to flashy restaurants with sea views, but this didn't help to move things on. He was tormented by the question of what to do in this situation. And by the question: why?

Yes, the question of encryption bothered him – he studied the Bible, he analysed the associated mass of records left by the Greeks and Jews, describing how they saw apparitions of Jesus and the reactions of different sections of society to this, and he came to the following conclusions:

a. the majority of the stories described in the Bible were exaggerated, initially with good intentions, in order to introduce an element of the epic and grand scale, and to surround the legends with an even greater aura of mystery and the supernatural; for at that time the market for religious stories was geared towards epic sagas, be they Norse, Roman or Greek. Jesus himself, resurrected after his death and seated beside his Heavenly Father, reminds us of Hercules at the very least; and if you compare it to a Norse epic, where those who perish in battle are taken to Valhalla by the Valkyries, maybe this, in some way, is what was actually being played out in the crucifixion of Christ, where the three Marys were beside Jesus, beholding his pain and suffering and the taunting of the crowd. Afterwards the stories were distorted for the benefit of the administrators of the Holy Church, so that they could conduct a programme for the humbling of the soul – or in other words, control the population, who put their faith in what was written.

b. The massive scale of the spread of the new faith can be attributed to at least three factors: Firstly, given the multitude of Gods who were revered in Rome, and given the fact that the empire was snowballing to hitherto unknown dimensions (and this opened the floodgates economically, for vast amounts of money were being poured down the drain, as they say nowadays, in maintaining an inefficient state apparatus and indulging the elite), the attitude to temples, gods, goddesses and demi-gods began to take on a formal character. And a formal attitude to religion is always a syndrome, a sign of the impending decay of civilisation. If the Gods cannot control the people, what is there to fear? What is the point of obeying? New Gods were needed, but there was no compelling concept – in other words, there were the Jews, with their Eternal One, who didn't particularly strive to expand their spiritual assets abroad and generally lived in a fairly segregated fashion, and then there were the other polytheists … pagans. The world demanded change, particularly the Roman World. This is what it wanted, and it found the answer in the lands of Palestine.

If the Christian movement had just been left as an idiosyncratic phenomenon within the confines of Judaea, nobody would have given it any thought today, apart from the historians! The broad expansion was guaranteed by the limitlessness of the Empire itself, the thousands of people living there in those times. It was very similar to the later contagion of the people by the utopian ideas of socialism and equality, which led the Reds to power in a different empire – the Russian one, which also extended over a pretty large territory. But that took place much later and was not so interesting, although quite bloody and dramatic, for sure!

Secondly, there was the social inequality in the Empire. The high prices for everything sold on the free and not-so-free market; the law that worked for friends, for the elite… but frequently did not work for the worse-off strata of society. And, of course, the huge amount of slave labour, which enabled the elite to obtain and accumulate excessive profit. These were people shipped out of the Roman colonies with other world views, other cultures, degraded by Rome, wrenched from their homes, caught up in the machinery of this corporation of monsters; people without roots, who hated, despised and feared Rome, and who wanted and did not fear change. This was fertile soil for planting a new religion. The religion of the poor. The religion of those appealing for equality and brotherhood.

See, once again, how many parallels can be drawn with the ideology of the Bolsheviks in Russia! A religion for the poor was needed, since the religion of the wealthy only secured the rights and defended the interests of the ruling class and the business elite, as they say nowadays. Slave owners were protected by "their God(s)". Slaves were forcibly taken from their lands, from their Gods, and they did not want to believe in the Roman Gods. They wanted to believe in their own, or rather to perform their rituals and honour their Gods with sacrifices – something which was, is and ever shall be the mark of distinction of any religion – but they were not given any opportunity. As a result, the slaves were prepared to sacrifice themselves to gain freedom and faith for their children, their own faith…and it was explained to them that this really was possible, that freedom was found in faith, inside yourself – just look at this actual example!

The third factor, the development of trade and shipping, along with the illiteracy of the majority of the Empire's population, gave the opportunity for an onslaught. Remember that after the death of the Saviour, his disciples created a network. Yes, really – a network, secret gatherings of the first Christians, persecuted and annihilated at that time by Roman officialdom. They gave sermons to the people on the fringes of the Roman Empire, where the authorities looked at it from a commercial point of view – "a couple of charlatans are going to hold a meeting, so what? Lots of people are good for the shopkeepers – and the shopkeepers pay us, not Rome!"

The network made miracles possible! For, Mr Ironson reasoned, the death of one poor and unremarkable craftsman could not become the catalyst for global change, even death on the cross, which was reserved solely for criminals…and even given that there existed a certain, albeit modest, number of followers (if you take into account the Empire and the number of its inhabitants) of those ideas which Yeshua (as the Jews addressed him) held and preached. But the thing is, a grain grows into an ear of wheat. The ear sheds its grain, and the following year produces three to five shoots from the grains which fell from that first ear and sprouted on the spot.

And after that – you've got a field already! Or fields, covering the land.

Mr Ironson was convinced that there was a configuration of numbers and/or signs which enabled those first shoots of wheat to survive in uncultivated soil and to leave a great legacy. To give something from which fields of wheat would later grow to feed the peoples of the world! Immortality, you could say, looking at the thousands of years which have passed since counting began.

Geoff Ironson was absolutely sure that everything, any event on this Earth, could be explained by mathematics. Figures, numbers... a system for controlling numbers, that's what he was interested in. He loved big numbers but was not averse to working out small problems. Once again – large numbers are derived from the modification of prime and small numbers.

Four

Side streets – dark, narrow – all around. Geoff saw himself walking barefoot, with the moon lighting his path intermittently. There were no signs to identify where all this could be taking place...

Maybe it was Valetta, or maybe Jerusalem, or...no, it was definitely some eastern city. It seemed to him that it was the East, but not the Far East, not Indochina or even the Indian subcontinent. It was the Near East or Southern Europe, the Maghreb...well, somewhere in those parts, although it's impossible to say for sure!

First, Geoff met Qbira and was not happy about the meeting. The Don was pensive and looked tired. His disappearance had evidently not done him any good. His eyes were hollow, and on his throat, where you usually find the Adam's apple, there was a gaping hole, from which some sort of sea creatures kept peeping out and disappearing back inside again. One minute a hermit crab, then a starfish.

He smiled a bitter sort of smile and at a salutatory nod from Geoff, opened his mouth and some words came out, but in a voice that was not like the voice of the living Don: "And where have you stashed the chest? Bring me the key, kid."

Geoff flinched, because Don Giovanni really did use to call him kid, while he was alive. And it must be said that Geoff hadn't liked it, but was forced to put up with it. And he put up with it now. Don Qbira slipped into the alleyway and disappeared behind some rubbish bins. A Moor came out and approached Geoff. He smiled and held out his hand, from which handcuffs were dangling with a cut chain. Geoff smiled at him and also held out his hand. At that moment he noted that the Moor's face was dotted as if with pock marks or tattoos. They were people: women, men and children, snaking over the Moor's face as if alive; they were holding their hands out in front of them as if begging for something.

Geoff touched just the fingertips of the Moor and felt a burning sensation; it became painful and there was a smell of scorched meat. He glanced at his fingers and saw that the tips were glowing red and smoking. The Moor smiled in response, but there was an evil glint in his eyes. The little people on his cheeks and forehead were now imploring Ironson, but he took no heed. He was terrified and wanted to get out of there.

The chain on the handcuffs began to unravel and tried to attack Geoff, coiling round him like a snake. He cried out in what sounded to him like the strange screech of a bird. Like a crow or something, and flapping his arms, he leaped back. Amazingly, he seemed to gain the ability to levitate, and by flapping his arm-wings he landed up in a place where he felt safe. It was a fortress wall, an ancient structure. The moon illuminated the sea, the wall and Geoff himself a little, although for some reason he shied away from the light, as if he was frightened of being seen.

He gazed at the moon, sitting on the edge of the wall and feeling like a crow. He looked at the celestial body as a bird would do, his head cocked slightly to one side. There were stars out there, beyond the moon, and they started to whirl in a round dance. It culminated in the stars turning into little tadpoles and then human embryos. They were slimy and seemed to be smiling. Then the moon exploded and began to drop down into the sea in pieces as it disintegrated, and the embryos vanished into the sky. He himself was carried by the waves and he cried out for help. Darkness fell. Geoff Ironson woke up in bed, in the room he had taken in one of Valetta's most expensive hotels. He lay in silence for some time, rubbing his eyes. Then he got up and went to answer a small call of nature – for even billionaires have to pee! He drank some water and got back into bed. His watch showed 02:11. Mr Ironson yawned, turned over on his side and dropped back to sleep for a little while – this time without any adventures.

Five

"What's up, mister, can't you sleep?"

The fisherman was sitting on the edge of his boat. It was early in the morning, and after a stressful night, full of strange dreams, Geoff had gone out for a walk. Dawn had hatched out from the egg of the East. It was cool outside, and it was coming up to 5am when the billionaire Ironson stepped outside his hotel. It took him just over ten minutes to reach the jetty where the boat was, amongst others of its kind.

Geoff looked at the fisherman and asked: "And how did you know that I speak English?"

"How could I not know? It's obvious! I see a lot of people around here, mister. Well, you're definitely not Italian, even less so, German – and you're not Russian, though you look a bit like it. You're American!"

"True, true. I'm from America," answered Geoff. "What's your name?"

"Luca. And you?"

"I'm Geoff."

They shook hands and Geoff saw a tattoo on the fisherman's wrist depicting a snake, pierced by a sword. The snake was some-what similar to the chain on the handcuffs the Moor was wear-ing in his dream last night. Geoff winced, although he did not want to offend his new acquaintance.

The fisherman just shrugged his shoulders and smiled.

"So, what are you doing here, Geoff? Are you a tourist? Why have you come down to the sea so early? Are you looking for something?"

"Sort of," replied the American. "I'm looking for an Order."

The fisherman smiled at him and said, "Well there's only one Order here, Mr Geoff. And there's no need to look for it, it's all around you."

"I never thought of that, Luca! There's another one here but I can't find any trace of it. Yesterday my lawyers hounded everyone, including local underworld dealers, but all traces are hidden in the water, as they say, at sea. One is dead, another emigrated and died abroad, a third ended up in prison for a minor offence and was found hanged there. It's a mystery − there is an Order, but no followers!"

"What Order, Mr Geoff? What's this association called? Maybe I can point you in the right direction."

Geoff smiled at the fisherman.

"If angels and demons couldn't help… oh, what the hell, let's give it a try. Have you heard of the Renunciates?"

The fisherman grinned.

"Have I heard of them?! I have direct contact with them Mr Geoff. Looks like you've come to the right place."

"Holy shit! Oh, sorry Luca − but could you introduce me to the head of your Order? I need − I desperately need to ask him a question which has really been bugging me. I'm sure he won't mind talking to me. If it's a question of money…"

"Stop, stop. Mr Geoff. Forget about money − just look at you − you need something, and you immediately grab for money. And if you were all alone at sea, amidst the waves, how would your money help you? What would you buy there? Some fish, perhaps…?" He laughed and set off a coughing fit. "I will try to set up a meeting for you, but promise me that you won't investigate any further."

"Yes, I promise, as soon as the working day begins, I'll call off the lawyers. They will stop, but…um… what sort of proof have you got that you really are a member of this Order?"

The Maltese rummaged in his pocket for cigarettes and matches. He struck one. A cloud of smoke was followed by more coughing.

"OK, I'll show you, but promise me you won't tell anyone at all about the details of our meeting, at least until you leave Malta. I think I can trust you – you look like the perfect gentleman."

"Luca, I make deals that would pay for all the property on your island. I know how to keep my mouth shut and I stick to my word."

"Ha–ha…" the fisherman laughed. "You mean to say someone's offering for you to buy all the property around here?"

"No, I'm not trying to," said Geoff, "I just wanted to demonstrate the scale on which you can trust me."

"Ah, I deal every day with a scale by comparison with which your business is nothing! Every day I go out to sea, and if anyone is wealthy in this world, it's the sea. How many fish, how many treasures are hidden away in its depths! And I can tell you, the sea is my old friend, but I don't trust it at all, in spite of its scale…I've learned from experience. But OK, I'll take you at your word. We'll see…"

He climbed into the little fishing boat, took out a leather bag and retrieved a piece of paper. The paper turned out to be a document which had been issued to someone back in 1866 and was sealed with the coat of arms of the Order – two rams standing on their hind legs and holding ears of corn and fruit in baskets. Below, under the rams' feet, a needlefish wound like a ribbon, and behind it was engraved the Order's motto: "Renunciation in His name". Behind the rams, beyond the horizon, the sun was rising. The rams represented the lamb, the sacrifice in the name of life. Ears of corn and fruit – the fruits of the earth. The sun – light, God's grace. The needlefish represented the power of the sea, fluidity of life, and its predatory nature, for the needlefish is a predator.

So here were the concepts of the Order itself, about which so little was known! Geoff knew that the principal idea was the renunciation of the academic God, as established in the small number of documents that had survived to this day, and recognition of the true, omnipresent God. Members of the Order were not noted in political or business circles, and since the membership had been declining through the centuries, they did not present any particular interest to the powers that be… and this Order could probably be called the "Order of the Poor". Moreover, in order to maintain its identity, and to put it bluntly, survive (since the established church anathematised this movement, and all followers who fell into the hands of the sovereign's people were executed or tortured to death in prison), the Order led a secretive existence. From its beginnings in 1688, counting from the Birth of Christ, the existence of the Order had always been under threat of physical destruction.

The seal and its depiction were genuine, and Geoff, who could not get over the shock of this chance meeting, knew it.

He nodded his head to signify his acceptance of the evidence presented, though he did not even attempt to read what was written, and simply asked (knowing that membership of the Order passed down through the family from generation to generation), "Who was this? Your grandfather?"

"My great-grandfather," replied Luca. "He was killed."

"I'm sorry," Ironson sighed sympathetically.

"Yes, the storm was fierce, and he was out at sea. He was hungry, so he put out to sea, not frightened of anything. We have to find our own food, we are strictly prohibited from accepting gifts or charity in situations when we are able to fend for ourselves."

"Well…you are certainly different from other associates of yours."

"It's not down to us. We just follow the covenant. They – all those others – broke the covenant, for they started to worship gold and their comforts, and got in with the big boys of this world, and you should never, ever do that, Mr Geoff."

"Why do you say that?"

"Because money is power, and power corrupts. As soon as you sit down with the princes of this world, you are in the networks of power, so we don't dance to order, and the Vatican is not our boss. What the Almighty gives us is a lack of human power and so, as you see – I'm a fisherman and you are a wealthy gentleman, but that doesn't bother me. And it turns out that the likes of me can actually help someone like you!"

"Very interesting! So, when can I meet your boss?"

"OK, Geoff, come to the jetty at half past four this afternoon and we'll go for a ride. I'll take you to see him. But please, don't pester him with too many highbrow questions and long words – he's an old man, and old men like to keep things simple."

"Great. I'll be here at four-thirty."

"OK, see you then," said Luca the fisherman, and he started up the motor in the boat.

The sun dial showed five forty in the morning, or somewhere approaching six. By fishermen's standards, it's ridiculously late to set out to sea, but you never know when you'll be lucky when it comes down to it.

Six

The old man was neat and tidy, a little reclusive and smelled of fried fish and cheap tobacco. You would never have imagined that the head of a secret Order would hide himself away in a tiny little room in a small fish market, where he worked as a cleaner!

There were only a dozen or so tables on which the fruits of the sea were displayed, and his task was to wash the tables down before the fishermen's wives set out their wares, just recently the property of the sea.

And after the women had left the market, he went in and cleaned the tables and swept up. It was dusty work in the sense that the dust remained there regardless, but it was not the greatest burden for an old man such as this Vincenzo.

He knew that a guest was coming, and he set out some wine, salad, bread and cheese for the meeting. The three of them barely squeezed into the room, which was the head-quarters – if you can call it that – of the Order of the Renunciates.

All this reminded Geoff of some kind of farce: an old man who cleans up after the tradeswomen and can barely support himself; a fisherman with an ancient certificate! It was like Don Quixote and his trusty Sancho, tilting at windmills! Deep down, Mr Ironson was disappointed, but he put on the appearance of being extremely interested.

Luca spoke in Maltese and Vincenzo listened – attentively, it seemed. He nodded his head to show he understood and was taking the guest's visit seriously. Then he said something in his slightly rasping old man's voice and waved his hand towards the food and wine, indicating that it wouldn't be a bad idea to entertain themselves, and then they could have a chat.

Having drunk a glass of wine (the glasses were clean, incidentally, otherwise Geoff would have refrained) and eaten a bit of cheese and fresh coriander, Mr Ironson discovered, to his surprise, that the food was really rather good, and the wine completely surpassed all expectations. A great little dry white, it would seem that one of the locals had made it for himself rather than general resale, for it was exceptional in its purity and flavour.

"I've told him about you, Mr Geoff," said Luca. "He is prepared to listen to you."

"I'm grateful for the opportunity to meet Mr Vincenzo in person. So, is he the cardinal of the Order?" Geoff asked the fisherman.

"No, we don't have cardinals. He is the keeper of the covenant. We call him the elder. And I assist him if and when necessary. Today it is necessary. We are the only two left, he and I – we are last of the Order on this earth."

"So, could he tell me something about the covenant? What sort of covenant is it?"

The fisherman translated the gist of the conversation. The old man Vincenzo poured himself some wine and began to speak in short sentences so that Luca would be able to translate them into English.

"In the beginning was the Word, which means the superiority of intellect. Without the Word we would have remained animals.

And this is one of the few truths to have been preserved in the Bible, in its official form, unchanged to this day. The first test of the Word was an angel. He extolled intellect over faith to the Holy Father. And we all know what happened next, don't we!

"The second test of the Word was people. Some people realised that the Word could be used as a weapon to give them superiority over others. That's how the clergy came about.

"Then things only got worse until the prophets began to appear – in spite of the fact that they defended the clergy in many respects, these people continued to speak and act from the heart. Many of them were killed."

Geoff found the conversation interesting but couldn't for the life of him hear the answer to his question.

"That's a very interesting interpretation," he said to Luca. "But all the same, what sort of covenant is it?"

The fisherman translated the question again and the old man, washing down some cheese with a drink, answered:

"The covenant is very simple: you have to go forth and multiply, you have to maintain purity and simplicity in body and soul and make what you will of your life. Nothing more. To go forth and multiply would seem pretty straightforward – however, it doesn't just mean the continuation of the human race, but also the reproduction of livestock, fish, gardens... it means nature, which bears fruit for you, mankind. Well, without the grape we wouldn't be able to drink wine, would we?!"

Geoff Ironson nodded and took a sip from his glass.

"The body and soul need to be kept clean and pure. In the literal sense, insofar as it relates to the body. As far as the soul is concerned, you must do as the prophets did. Follow your heart – they didn't leave us commandments, but the human heart stores all this knowledge inside. We are connected by this world, so why do something that contradicts the heart and then look for reasons and have doubt in the Creator?"

"Yes, it's a fairly straightforward approach to complex issues," said Geoff, smiling. "But wasn't it important for the congregation to have moral boundaries? For if it is as you say, they need to control themselves and make their own choices – but not everyone is able to do that, are they?"

Luca translated what he said to Vincenzo, who, after a short pause to chew some bread, replied:

"Yes, simplicity is one of the basic criteria for existence. The world is not as complicated as people make out. It is multifaceted, there will always be joy and sorrow, lies and truth, but this is intrinsic to the nature of the World. Look at the fish in the sea – they have learned to deceive predators – is that not lying? But they can't let the predators destroy their race, so what else are they supposed to do? They are not stronger or faster or more intelligent than their predators, but over the period of their existence they have discovered the weakness of their enemy and they make use of it. Some sort of weakness… a shortcoming. And that's how it all works.

"As for moral boundaries, God has given us reason and faith. Man's task is to develop both of these and balance them inside himself. Read the Bible – is it not an amoral book if you read it carefully? So many examples of people's mistakes and stupidity…"

Geoff stopped to think for a minute, then asked: "And what do you know about the code? The code of life?"

Vincenzo smiled. "Luca, you remember that anyone who has ever come to us from outside, as far as I can recall, has asked about the code of life. Last time, about two years ago, a Russian poet came here, looking for the meaning and the code. They say he got married shortly afterwards and stopped searching.

"And you, mister, do you know what they say about the number of the Beast?"

Geoff nodded to confirm that he knew.

"And what do three sixes look like, mister?"

"Like three sixes," Mr Ironson smiled in response.

"They look like three people whose bellies are full of food, for they have only been concerned with finding nourishment for themselves that day. And their heads are bowed because they are weighed down with thoughts of how to make money to buy food.

"These three are faith, hope and love." The old man looked craftily at Geoff. "Now do you understand, mister?"

"No, not exactly," said Mr Ironson.

"So, it's true what they say about Americans – they have brains but can't be bothered to think!"

They all laughed at the joke, even Mr Ironson.

"No, of course I overdid the bit about faith, hope and love. I lied to you, Mr Geoff! Will you have some more wine?"

"Just a little... thank you."

"Well, there isn't a lot left. We'll soon be able to see the bottom of the flagon…it'll be empty before you've finished saying what you wanted to say!

"So those three are the muses of man. This is the beginning. Whatever you say, we were made as creators, but we became slaves. So, who is the creator?" He again looked at his guest, through narrowed eyes.

"The child is the creator. If you turn the sixes around, they become nines. And they are like human embryos still inside the womb. Three of them – faith, hope and love. The muses of the world."

Geoff took a sip of wine and asked: "And what does it give a person, the possession of this knowledge? How does this code help?"

"It will give the person what he needs," replied the old man. "You play at your games, Mr Geoff, and I play at mine. What do you need in order to remain a child? You have to avoid burdening yourself with cares, or rather, avoid rating your everyday concerns over the freedom of the spirit. For the third commandment of the covenant regards creation."

"You can't create without any concerns!" Geoff said to the old man. "I also create in a sense. My company is very large, and I employ almost eighteen thousand people on three continents. But there are plenty of concerns, and if I don't take care of them, who will?"

"Well, there are concerns and then there are concerns."

He said something to Luca, who rummaged around in a corner and found something long, wrapped in fringed cloth. He handed it to the old man. Vincenzo opened the bundle and pulled out a pipe, a wooden reed pipe.

He raised it to his lips and played a few practice notes, but it was clear that the audience was waiting for a performance.

The old man played for two or three minutes. Something quite light-hearted at first, and then a rather more melancholy tune. Putting the instrument down, he drank the remains of the wine and said to Geoff: "So that's it, Mr Geoff. Now you can go back to America and concern yourself with your major transactions. I'm tired now and I've had a lot to drink. I need to go and rest."

"But what is the code? Is everything really so meaningless?!"

"It really is," grimaced the old man. "And it's true that you people really do have small brains. Farewell Mr Geoff. All the best."

"Goodbye," Geoff answered sadly, in a slightly hurt voice.

And only when he was in the sky above the Atlantic did the meaning of what had taken place suddenly dawn on him. Music! That was the code. Everyone carries music inside themselves and plays according to their own ability. Everyone plays out their own life like a piece of music. We are all reed pipes of the Almighty… Geoff smiled at the metaphor that resounded in his head.

Seven

"I have a question for you, Mr Ironson," said S. Iblis, looking into the eyes of his visitor, who had made himself comfortable in the armchair of his office. "Were you satisfied with your trip?"

"Extremely," answered Geoff.

"And what did you find out specifically that satisfied you? None of our firm's efforts brought any tangible results. It looks as if the Order has died out over the past two or three decades. Or do you know something we don't?"

"Mr Iblis, let me answer your question with a question."

"Ok, I'm listening!"

"Do you play any sort of musical instrument?"

Mr Iblis smiled and answered, "Yes, I play many instruments. It's enjoyable and gratifying, don't you think, Mr Ironson?"

"Yes, I agree. I also play, in a way…"

"Oh, I understand you Geoffrey! So that means you found what you were looking for?"

"I've just opened the door a crack."

"Well, be careful – there could be anything at all behind that door, have you thought of that?"

"No, I haven't. But you seem to be a bit of an authority on the subject, is that right?"

"I have an in-depth knowledge of the subject, as you have accurately observed," laughed S. Iblis. "I would go so far as to say that in a certain way, I suffered because I wanted to know more and more."

"Then I have another question for you, as an authority."

"Go ahead, I'm all ears!"

"Why Christ in particular, and why that particular code?"

"That's a long debate, Mr Ironson. I think I know the answer and could condense it into a few sentences rather than waste time on long explanations.

"Well, it's likely that the one who was crucified by the people…was attempt number two. He was a soldier – whatever they've written about him – he was an uncompromising soldier, and they made a figurehead out of him. But that's typical of mankind!"

"But then who was attempt number one?" enquired Ironson.

"The first attempt was the one who was defeated for reason and beauty – however strange that may seem. He was an artist, in the image of the Creator, and they turned him into the Devil. That's also typical of mankind. Basically, if it hadn't been for the first attempt, there wouldn't have been a second – but that's just my speculation!

"As I see it, both these attempts failed as experiments. Let's not go into the reasons now, but people needed to believe.

"If you remember, people believed in fire, thunder, snowstorms – in things that don't die forever in death – and it was necessary to give gifts to the Gods in the form of sacrifices… So, it turned out that what seemed like a loss-making enterprise, to put it in business terms, suddenly brought unbelievable dividends. But there was only one beneficiary…" The narrator pointed to the sky. "As for the code, what more can you suggest that isn't already covered by 'so it was and so it shall be, and there is nothing new under the sun'?

"What is really unique is this collection of sounds – nobody knows where they originate, nobody knows how they enter into this world and they linger here only briefly – because it's wonderful. And what is pleasing, Mr Ironson, is that everyone has his own music! The music of the soul has no bounds – it is important not to play out-of-tune, but each according to his ability. On that note, so to speak, we must end this chat. Business calls, you know…"

"Yes, of course! I understand."

"I hope you were happy with our service, Mr Ironson."

"Absolutely, Mr Iblis. I am going to play my music. Thank you for your time and elucidation. The account has been settled, have you checked?"

"Oh, don't worry about that! I don't get worked up about the settlement of accounts," Mr Iblis smiled in response. "That's something I'm totally confident about – if not today, then tomorrow!"

Geoff went out, leaving Iblis on his own.

He sat deep in thought for a while, then dialled a number on his mobile.

"Can I speak to Aiz Aizell?"

"Yes, just a moment, Mr Iblis," replied a pleasant woman's voice.

"Hey, Mr Iblis, in the flesh!" he heard Aiz's clear voice.

"Aiz, old man," Samael said to him, "I need to take care of a client. Nothing personal, you understand, but he's sniffed out the code and it seems he is seriously carried away with the idea of the freedom of spirit. Well, as you can understand, there are certain risks."

"Shall I take down his name?"

"Yes, put 'Geoff Ironson, head of the conglomerate 'Ai-Qbira'."

"OK, got it, boss! What do you want me to do?"

"Remove him. Best of all, do the same as with his former employer, Giovanni Qbira, if you remember."

"Ah, the fat guy – Qbira!" laughed Aiz.

"Yes, yes, that's the one."

"Leave it to me, Mr Iblis, boss!"

"OK and there's something else. You have specialists in this field… when you've finished with the man, give them a task – make them remove as much information as possible about him from the internet – and falsify the rest, or well, show the rather more dubious sides of the deceased's character. We're also going to have to find somebody more suitable for the role of managing Ai–Qbira, to stop these constant blunders with the senior management! Taxi drivers who are ready to govern states are ten a penny. Gangsters have now started to degenerate into sentimental romantics for political reasons, and you can't find a dispassionate manager, who can conduct business appropriately, for love nor money!"

"OK… I've written it down, so we have to wipe as much information about Mr Ironson as possible from the internet, and anything left there we make look a bit shady, right?"

"Yes, exactly. A bit shady!"

"OK, boss. Shall I get to work right away?"

S. Iblis thought for a moment. "Wait a couple of days. Today is Friday, start on Monday. Let the man enjoy the music of life for a bit."

"Understood, boss. Have a good weekend!"

"Bye, Aiz! Ciao."

Mr S. Iblis went over to the record player and ran his puffy white fingers over the vinyl discs in their covers, which were standing beside it. He pulled out a disc and after an initial performance of hissing and crackling, the voice of Del Monaco rang out: "Nessun dorma, Nessun droma, Tu pure, O Principessa!"

He liked what he heard. Nothing else interested him – only these sounds, which were tender and powerful. The flowers of darkness, splendid in their renunciation of light, but at the same time terrible in their deadly beauty, blossomed within that being who bore so many names. "Music is probably the most successful of His experiments!" thought S. Iblis, looking at the spinning disc and listening to the final "All'alba vincero!"

Odessa, September 2016–June 2017

IN THE LAND OF THE GREE

Professor Giuseppe Grazzini led Mr Gardner through a network of corridors and told him the story.

"When all the major powers decided to form the World State – One World, set the World Government and elect the president, the main aims were to be chosen by the president elected. The first decision the World's new masters made was to combat poverty and clean up the environment. It was very humane and praised by all nations. After a joint action, combining hard scientific work and training, the World entered into a battle with pollution and waste.

"The basic Law had been developed and accepted, so it regulated the whole deal. Since Japan and Israel developed the technologies, others provided financing and machinery as well as maximum social support, training camps and equipment.

"On the seas, in particular, special vessels were developed and built in the shipyards of Korea and Japan and navigated all around the oceans, collecting the garbage on the high seas, and from the main ports. The program was paid from the budget and the budget was filled by the taxes, which are regularly payable by almost all the planet's businesses, as there were no longer offshore zones around, except for maybe a few rebel areas which were not yet part of the One World.

"There was a tender for an appropriate place for all the waste to be collected to get stored and recycled into energy and polyethylene. There were bids from few areas, but logistically and logically the choice fell to this African land. It is a desert here, as you can see. Almost a desert.

"Our family's business won the tender for the management of the whole deal. We have been in the garbage business since 1788, when my ancestors started it in Genoa, so we are the best professionals the World could have found!

"Well, here we are: it's the coordination desk. We coordinate the World's waste flow out of this room!

"Remember, as one of my grandfathers said to me once: "If we do not take the waste off the ground promptly, Genoa will sink in its own shit in two weeks." So imagine, the same applies to the whole planet! We have to clean it constantly. No rest. Always at service!

"And people are happy as we know it," ended Giuseppe on a positive note.

Mr Gardner was looking at the room and studied some smart machinery with great interest. A large part of the job was done by robots. But then, indeed, the whole chain of waste collecting and delivery, waste flow information, coordination and recycling, employed a huge volume of professionals worldwide.

And it was good idea to have the place for storage and recycling here, at this remote African shore. In Europe or in the USA, there might have been many politicians trying to speculate and hurt the process.

This part of Africa, especially after the chain of deadly epidemics and wars, remained one of the World's zones where even the known and mighty multinational corporations were not keen to do business. So, indeed, the setting up of such business brought a bit of relief here and certainly some civilized consumption spirit.

"And how is it with the locals? How do they consider this project? Do you employ many of them?" came a question from the guest.

The Professor looked at Mr Gardner and responded with a slightly cynical tone "Mr. Gardner, if your land was a large base for the World's waste storage, would you be happy? I doubt it.

"And we cannot employ a lot of Africans here, because it demands extensive training and these people are lazy and unwilling to listen to us. But, as a sort of gift, we let them use the industrial garbage for… hm… their real estate, I would so call it. They benefit, because they can get a limited access to the storage center and select there anything they like, taking as much as they can carry with them to later equip their residential areas or use for other purposes."

"Uh, it smells a bit inhumane, to let them dig in the garbage! For me it is a point for a possible conflict, and I have to mention it in my report of course!" Mr Gardner said.

"Do not be hasty, Mr Gardner. Indeed, it looks ugly, but we took those risks seriously, especially the risks of rebellion, which may indeed happen. Or rather, it might have happened if we had not sorted things out here. True we've used a bit of deception, but better to deceive a little, rather than spill seas of blood," said the professor to the auditor, Jerome Gardner.

"Oh, interesting – what is your method, dear Giuseppe?" asked Jerome.

"We used the Bible. We threw them an idea that God has chosen their land to serve the cleaning of the Planet. There is something biblical over here, don't you think so?!

"We found appropriate lines in the Book and you know…

"Africans represent very religious communities and they were actually happy to accept us as messengers of God. They consider themselves the ones who provide us the shelter, and that is also an action of the Divine! The last auditor, Mr. MacDouglas, who was here prior to you and inspected the place, called it, after he learnt the full story, the "land of the gree".

"But as usual, a good deception is only good and acceptable if it contains a part of the truth at least. We are here for Good, that's for sure. Without our job, the whole Planet would sink in garbage. Isn't it a very special function, which may be coloured as a superior one and seen as an absolutely necessary one? And whatever job is an absolute necessity for everyone on this Planet, can be described as God's blessed business!" Giuseppe smiled.

They took a short trip using a small e-car down to the storage center. It was a huge mountain-like place full of garbage, surrounded by armed security points and barbed wire, where some local Africans were messing to grab a bit of civilisation's waste and carry it to their homes as Gifts of the Clean World.

Security guards were watching over them. Mr Gardner was surprised to detect a flag on top of the mound of garbage.

"What's that?" he asked.

"That's a propaganda flag, saying in several local languages *"This is the Land of Mastery, please do not waste it, in the name of the Lord!* It serves the purpose. As I said before, a bit of deception is never a great sin, if it is managed properly."

THE CASE OF LAST NIGHT'S DREAM (BUT THEN AGAIN...)

1:1. 31st October 2016, Halloween. I have begun to write these lines.

1:2. But then again: what difference can even a thousand pumpkins make? Or a thousand words, if they are as hollow as pumpkins? Several thousand years of constant struggle for a sweet pumpkin's worth of power?

1:3. I am trying to imbue the lines with meaning. I am trying to kick them into shape, to stop them lounging around idly on their rectangular white background. There's work to be done, do you hear?!

1:4. But then again: how could letters, or even whole sentences, possibly hear me? How could anyone be heard by a brick wall? Well, only if the person himself suddenly turned into a brick wall...then I suppose he could!

1:5. I have started to sleep better at night – I must be tired. There are things happening in my life that I don't understand. I am looking for answers. Hear me, oh Giver of Answers! Although sleep is so sweet, even without answers!

1:6. But then again: a half-eaten apple, already browned on one side, an empty glass, still reeking of vodka, and a stale piece of white bread – this is the still-life of this evening.

My laptop is open to me, and to the rest of the world, on the dining-room table. Food, drink and a screen...a system of giving and rewarding! A river, relentlessly changing the contours of its banks, over and over again; Sable Island – the ships' graveyard.

Something is glinting on the other side of the river. It looks like some sort of wild animal… an ass? Or maybe a startled deer? There are symbols for every kind of life. But let's get back to reality: apple, alcohol and bread.

1:7. The air is pierced with anxiety. Rumours of a better life have dissolved in the holy wine. The facts, that life is getting harder, flit before our eyes – like gnats. Bloody gnats!

1:8. But then again: of course, there's no Halloween without the devil! But what kind of spirit of darkness can break or defile a person born in the USSR? That was done long ago by the delegates of Communist Party congresses and their present-day successors – aggravated by TV advertising and the daily scramble for consumer satisfaction. It was done by the symbolic worker and state-farm girl. It was done by the children in the yard, who wouldn't let you look at their magazine full of photos of male and female genitals, ejaculating and receiving sperm. It was done by the youths taking attractive young girls, drunk and exuding lust… away from you on a summer's night.

1:9. Hold on! Time isn't rushing anywhere. Listen to your heart beating. You're the one rushing. It's the hands on your clock moving forward, not time. Time is a commodity – we exchange it for life in the hope of gain. We are in a hurry to exchange something we don't have – for something that has been granted us as a gift. We are hopeless dreamers and relentless bullshitters.

1:10. But then again: take a beggar rummaging in a dustbin. It is important for him to hurry – this is his moment! Otherwise, other stinking beggars will come along and steal his spoils. He has to hurry, he wants to control the situation; his hands are shaking, unable to hold on to his bundle of power. *Fascio,* as a certain Commander-in-Chief from the not too distant past would have said.

1:11. Night is drawing in. The water is gurgling in the heating pipe. A spider is sitting frozen in the corner – or maybe it's already dead. The room fills with sounds, it is pervaded by strange forms. My thoughts blossom like flowers of the darkness. These flowers will wilt by morning, turning to rubbish in my subconscious. I will wake up…or maybe I won't. Morning will come, as the ancients said…

1:12. But then again: attempts to justify your own cowardice always end up in memories of the past. Do I get frightened, remembering last night's dream? What if it was terrifying, prophetic… what if that dream was unbearably painful? What if it were to come true? Yes, I'm frightened! I'll probably be frightened.

I'm not sure that… Oh, to hell with it – the illusion doesn't end! The case of last night's dream is closed!

1:13. I fantasised about building a church. An unconventional one – it would be peaceful, with its ceiling in the form of a glass sphere, made from thick, green – no, emerald-coloured glass. This church would be like a lighthouse by the sea. And the beacon flaring beneath the dome would radiate, emitting its light, streaming out from the green-tinted glass. Inside, just one single word would be written, or engraved in stone, on the walls. Something like: *Haimanutha, Ipa, Imani, Fidi, Amanah…*

1:14. But then again: who needs that sort of temple? A dreamer's ego? A hungry, wise old man? A sailor stepping ashore? Lonely hearts? Why try to guess – just imagine it, with its simple décor, no silver or gold… and only one word all around. In the beginning was the word. Then people used the word and whole sentences appeared, then confused stories and parables. The simplicity of words was lost, since there became a need to complicate life. Parables can be used very successfully to hide important things that it is better not to know… "and you will be fishers of men", it was said to the fishermen-thieves – what do you make of that, for example?

1:15. The children are twittering like little birds. The forest of our home has come to life again. I'm ready for a rest.

1:16. But then again: what do you do for your children? Take them to school in the morning, bring them home again in the evening. Brief conversations of the type: "What did you do today? How did it go?" They love you, and there you are, building temples. You idiot. Aging, weary, trying to escape from reality. Yet in your childhood you could fly: nobody will believe you, but it's true. Try explaining that to your children. Try to teach them that! But it's easier not to go there…I have changed. I have grown up, I have foundered and every day I drink a little from my cup. A fine sort of dad I am!

1:17. The market is buzzing – it speaks in hundreds of languages. Rivers of poison flow into the ears of jabbering fools. Speechwriters are in great demand. They write for the men in suits, scribbling day and night. They can't miss out – the time is right, everything is on the edge of the abyss again, which means they can sell fear, exchange it for time, and time for life. Though not for everyone…

1:18. But then again: noise is interesting as a medium. If you switch it off it's like being in the realm of fish: everyone opens their mouths but not a sound is heard. They grimace, for they have to sell their goods, although the goods are poor quality as usual. But they have to sell now, otherwise the quality will only deteriorate. And the customers also go around with their mouths wide open and eyes full of determination; they pay their money to be cheated on the spot – but at such a good price! And that's the game – nobody expects to win, but it is so important for everyone to be part of the process.

1:19. Whoever he was, he saved a lot of souls – although he was probably the undoing of a fair number as well. Tell me, what was the name of the person who invented wine and taught others to drink it? That's the real saint-cum-devil!

1:20. But then again: the Greeks taught how to dilute it with water, complementing the alcohol with goat's cheese and olives. The French taught how to use it to seduce young girls, adding a drop of passion, with bubbles beating against the glass from inside the bottle. Noah taught his children that wine can lead to exposure; and how often do we come across exposed, drunken people on the streets – they reveal hitherto unheard-of stories of life, death, love and betrayal. And knowing the properties of wine, we turn away from this nakedness, although deep down inside we want to be the same – exposed and open to dialogue. But not many people can allow themselves openness to dialogue these days – loutishness has a greater following.

1:21. It is getting light. Morning is being painted in dark blue tones across the sky. It is quiet, the children are still asleep. I can hear their breathing close by. A waft of wind outside the window ruffles the silver birch tree's coiffure. Its leafy hair is coloured yellow, green and russet. It is falling, blown away by the wind. The wind carries it across the still empty side-streets of the village.

The children's breathing carries their young lives in their sleep, like leaves. Where does that comparison come from, you ask? Well, where do you come from? Where do any of us come from? We are all but leaves!

1:22. But then again: light fills the darkness and renders it transparent. Maybe we continue to walk in darkness, although it is disguised in light, like those autumn leaves – for they did not stop being leaves when they changed colour!? Otherwise, why do we have such an inexorable need for darkness, rest and sleep? The lesson of fading away and the lesson of awakening. The lesson of changing is truly a very important one!

Odessa, 31.10.2016

The author

Viktor Korobko was born and raised in Odessa and is married with four children. He began writing poetry in the 1990s and published his first novel in 2015. He has since published four more works and enjoys walking, cooking, and fishing.